Hugh Johnston

A Review of Rev. F.W. Macdonald's Life of Wm. Morley Punshon

Hugh Johnston

A Review of Rev. F.W. Macdonald's Life of Wm. Morley Punshon

ISBN/EAN: 9783337205942

Printed in Europe, USA, Canada, Australia, Japan

Cover: Foto ©Raphael Reischuk / pixelio.de

More available books at **www.hansebooks.com**

British American Bank Note Co Montreal

A REVIEW

OF

REV. F. W. MACDONALD'S LIFE OF

WM. MORLEY PUNSHON, LL.D.

BY

REV. HUGH JOHNSTON, M.A., B.D.

WITH AN

INTRODUCTION BY REV. GEO. DOUGLAS, LL.D.

AND AN

ESTIMATE OF THE GREAT PREACHER'S CHARACTER AND WORK IN CANADA,

By HON. SENATOR MACDONALD.

———◆———

TORONTO:

WILLIAM BRIGGS. 78 & 80 KING STREET EAST.

C. W. COATES, MONTREAL.   S. F. HUESTIS, HALIFAX, N.S.

1888.

INTRODUCTION.

———

"WHEN the last sunshine of expiring day,
   In summer's twilight weeps itself away ;
   Who hath not felt the softness of the hour
   Sink on the heart as dew along the flower ?
   Even as the tenderness that hour instils,
   When summer's day declines along the hills ;
   So feels the fulness of our heart and eyes
   When all of genius which can perish, dies."

Seldom in a generation, has a message flashed across the sea that awakened a wider thrill of sorrow among the thousands of this Dominion, than the intelligence that the tongue of the great orator was forever silenced on earth ; that England's most popular preacher had disappeared from the pulpits of the land ; that William Morley Punshon was dead.

Deep and lasting was the sense of irreparable loss, that no more should we sit under the spell of his magic power, and catch the inspiration to a nobler life, kindled by his matchless, his anointed eloquence.

And now, after a lapse of years, a feeling, akin to that of the poet, as he stood amid the shadows of the expiring day, comes over the heart, in the form of a subdued emotion, and a gentle regret, like the memories of melodies long departed; like the lingering fragrance of the shattered vase; like the touch of the vanished hand, and the sound of the voice that is still.

Replete with warmth of heart, and all the attributes which fit for choicest fellowship, the elect company who were admitted into the inner sanctuary of his friendship, who came under the spell of his personal fascination, would naturally cherish for him an imperishable recollection. Not, however, for this was Dr. Punshon a man of renown. It was his pulpit power, his resplendent eloquence, which made his name the synonym of all grace and charm in oratory.

While the pulpits of Christendom are gifted with ministers effective and potent; while the senate is adorned with statesmen that can debate the economies of the nation; and the bar rejoices in sons who expound the philosophies of justice, the gift of true eloquence is never the lavish endowment of many, but is restricted to the units in any generation.

The genius of eloquence is rare as that of the higher poetic faculty, or that intuitional power of thought, which ascends to altitudes beyond the reach of average intelligence. Now, it was this genius of eloquence which gave to the subject of this memoir, his unrivalled distinction, extending his name and his fame wherever the language of the Saxon is known. In the allotments of Providence, it has been given to the writer of this introduction, to hear most of the men distinguished for eloquence in the past and present generations:—Dr. James Dixon, philosophic, profound and sublime, whose illustrations were arguments, and an inspiration that the effacing finger of time could never impair.—Dr. Joseph Beaumont, whose enthusiastic soul rippled and rolled, and foamed, like the cataract, corruscated like the light, and, as winged lark (of which he loved to speak), soared and sang towards the heavenly.— Dr. Robert Alder, of imperial mien, the finest expositor of missions which God ever gave to

Methodism.—John Rattenbury, master of all
emotions, who, like the skilled musician, could
handle his audience as an instrument, dissolving
to tears, or waking to ecstasies.—Bishop Simpson, holding, as it seemed, the resources of the
universe in his keeping, who could garnish his
thought with the brilliance of his imagination,
fuse it with the white heat of his emotions, and
pour it forth with phenomenal effect upon the
multitudes.—Bishop Doggett, the pride of Virginia scholastic, yet impassioned and all-com-
prehending.—Bishop Thompson, the Chrysostom
of the American Church.—Dr. Thomas Eddy,
full of evidential power.—Thomas Binney, the
idol of London, whose conversational discourses
sparkled and blazed, like an intellectual firma-
ment, moulding the thoughts of thousands of the
finest young men of his age.—Henry Ward
Beecher, the Shakespeare of the modern pulpit,
whose depth of perennial thought and affluence
of simile will perpetuate his memory along the
years.—Dr. Stone, the Moore of the American
ministry, who still lingers in the sunny clime of
the El Dorado of the west.—Canon Henry Mel-

ville, the silver-tongued of St. Paul's.—Canon
Liddon, who, despite his churchly limitations,
reveals the potencies of logic, fired by a lofty
enthusiasm.—Dr. John Cumming, mellifluous as
the cadences of the Æolian harp, he seemed
to breathe prophetic of the coming millenium.—
Sálisbury, the Rupert of debate, amid the serene
frigidities of the House of Peers.—Gladstone,
the Demosthenes of our day, and the statesman
of all time.—Richard Cobden, the great com-
moner, who voiced the cry of famishing millions.
—Sumner, at once the Cicero and Solon of the
American Senate. — Ralph Waldo Emerson,
whose transcendental thoughts, set in poetic
beauty, were like apples of gold in pictures of
silver.—Agassiz, uncovering more of the think-
ings of God in simple, flowing style, than man
had ever done before.—Wendell Phillips, the
most statuesque and finished orator this continent ever gave to a great cause.—Signor
Gavazzi, who carried the unity of Italy, by the
inspiration of speech, as truly as Garibaldi did
by the inspiration of his name.

These, and many others, which time and space

forbid us to name, we have heard in some of their most inspired moments. The majority have gone into the eternal, but their record abides, telling of peerless power of thought, and the attributes of all oratorical resource.

It would, of course, be unfair, and, indeed, untrue, to rank the subject of this memoir with those princes in the realm of thought and expression; nevertheless, we hesitate not to assert, that, in his own sphere, he was the compeer of them all. For power, by an alchemy all his own, to transmute our language into jewelled sentences,.clear and crystalline as the diamond, opulent in all beauty as the opal, and exquisite as the tints of the amethyst; for power of sustained brilliance of climax, of ringing intonation on a single word; for power to take hold of familiar truth, and robe it in a rhetoric, that made it a charm and a delight, alike to Romanist, to sceptic, and to worldling; for power to handle the rod, which, in his hands, budded into beauty, like that of an Aaron; for power to pierce the conscience with the shafts of truth, albeit, garlanded and hidden in flowers, though they be;

for power to bring the music and magnetism of the orator to exalt and thrill, Dr. Punshon stood unrivalled in his generation.

But peerless as were his powers of oratory, his Christian character gave strength and dignity to his rhetoric.

Before the coming ministry of Methodism, he stands as an illustrious example of diligence, in the culture of his powers, in loyalty to the Church of his choice, in fidelity to the cardinal truths of Methodist theology, and in a consecration which laid his every power on the altar of service for the Master Divine.

If doubts he had, Dr. Punshon never ventilated those doubts. He renounced utterly, and despised the shallow artifice of those who, to win a vitiated popularity, affect superiority in mental calibre; pretending to a breadth of thought, of culture, and of mock originality, which disdains loyalty to the formulæ of accepted truth; who seek to astonish the ignorant with emasculating views of inspiration; who proclaim, as novelties, the worn out dogmas of Socinianism, that the Christian atonement means nothing but the moral

influence which comes from a spectacular effect
of martyred innocence. He knew nothing of
the larger hopes, and *post mortem* probations,
because he failed to authenticate such from the
teachings of Scripture.

While his memory lingers in the churches, this
shall be his crown of unfading honour; that he
was faithful to the authority of Scripture, and
to the form of sound words, which he had received through the ministries of Methodism.

The advent and career of Dr. Punshon in
Canada, we always associate with that of an
oratorio—rare and beautiful. In every pulpit
he struck notes that will vibrate in minds forever; on every platform he took up refrains that
will linger in the heart's remembrance, like some
sweet sonata. And what were his lectures, but
the jubilates of his power. His " Call of An-
drew," the discourse with which he opened his
Canadian ministry in Montreal; his " Conflict
of Laodicea," which signalized the Kingston
Conference; his appeal to " Pulpit and Pew,"
which made notable the Toronto Conference;
the magnificence of his address to the Bible So-

ciety of Montreal; his lecture on the "Huguenots," most brilliant of all his productions; and his anointed and closing discourse on the "Apocalyptic vision of the prayers of saints"—epochs were these, in the mental history of all who shared in the rapture of the occasions, which, alas, will come no more.

No candid mind can peruse the pages that will follow, without rising to the conviction that Canadian Methodism stands forever indebted to the influence of William Morley Punshon.

The tale of his achievement, in giving elevation to its ministry, and recognition to its membership over all the land, will be transmitted by sire to son, from the Laurentides that guard the golden gateway of this Dominion, to the everglades that listen to the tidal music, that, faint and low, beat upon our further shore.

As autumnal tints glorify and veil the deformities of approaching death, as the white robe which envelops our land hides all decay, and stands as the symbol of all purity, to be followed by the resurrection of a coming springtime; so the grandeur of Dr. Punshon's life-work

encircled and flung its radiance over his departure.   His stainless character, of purest white,
shall endure until the resurrection morn, when
we hope to clasp hands on the banks of eternal
deliverance.   Till then :

> " His good deeds, through the ages,
>   Living in historic pages,
>   Will brighter glow and gleam immortal,
>   Unconsumed by moth and rust."

GEORGE   DOUGLAS.

WESLEYAN THEOLOGICAL COLLEGE,
    Montreal, April 3rd, 1888.

CONTENTS.

Contents.

ILLUSTRATIONS.

W. MORLEY PUNSHON, LL.D.

I.

THERE is nothing more precious and worthy in literature than biographical writings. The study of history is most important; it is the study of man. Biography is the study of the greatest of men, the men that influence the age in which they live, the men who make history. True, the course of human events is not shaped by great men alone. There is no earnest work of the humblest toiler

> " That is not gathered, as a grain of sand
> To swell the sum of human action, used
> For carrying out God's end."

We need to be kept from what is called hero-worship—

> " Pay not thy praise to lofty things alone,
> The plains are everlasting as the hills."

.Yet, if humanity sums up entire nature and represents it, then great and gifted men in their turn sum up and represent humanity. This is why biography instructs and charms us. There is in every life an image of our deepest self. In each noble deed done, and courageous battle fought, we feel an influence that is helpful, and whatever the struggles and successes, the failures and defects, we are reminded by them of our own. The lives of the great and good in all ages are our richest heritage, and the memorials of them embodied in permanent literature, they continue to shed a brighter and holier influence over the world. Especially is this true of those who have bequeathed to the Church of God the legacy of exalted virtues, consecrated gifts and apostolic labours, for "the righteous shall be in everlasting remembrance." Ever since the death of William Morley Punshon, there has been an eager longing for some more intimate memorial of one, the lustre of whose name will never, never perish from the annals of Methodism—a name suggestive of unrivalled eloquence wherever it is known and pronounced.

This long-felt want is now met in the delightful memorial volume, by Rev. F. W. Macdonald, who has been aided in his labour of love by Professor Reynar, of Victoria University, he having furnished the chapters which refer to Dr. Punshon's life in Canada.

The book is dedicated in brotherly affection and esteem to the younger ministers of Methodism on both sides of the Atlantic. In his preface, the author expresses regret that the publication has been so long delayed, and hopes that the delay has not been altogether prejudicial, for it has given time for the acquisition of ampler biographic material, and to the writer the perspective of a few years. The biographer seriously felt that in giving a measured estimate of Dr. Punshon's rank as a preacher and orator, the "personal equation" was a disturbing one. The spell of his eloquence, and the aroma of his spirit were yet over us; the memories of his rare rich ministry were yet too fresh with us all, and the sorrow over his untimely death still unassuaged; so the friend-critic must wait the lapse of years for calm, and acute, and discriminating judgment. The reading public, whose grateful favour he has challenged by this memorable work, will no doubt accept the author's apology for the long delay in the appearance of the book ; but, for my part, I should have preferred it sooner, even though the biographer had been compelled to carry less the tone and manner of a "faculty."

Few biographers have had more abundant materials placed at their disposal, in the shape of letters, private journals, notes of travel, newspaper records carefully preserved, printed documents, and published lectures, poems and sermons, and out of these the hand of the scholar and thinker, with a rare insight into character, and with subtle, delicate feeling, has made a portraiture worthy the transcendently-gifted man, whose life he delineates. When Phidias, the artist, was changing the marble block into a beautiful and majestic human form, he despised no implement or operation, however slight, which could in any way contribute to the perfection of that intended form. So, the eminent Professor of Theology, realizing

the personal importance belonging to the subject, has spared no pains to bring to the highest
degree of excellence this wonderful and noble
biography.

There is a breadth and richness of culture, a
literary finish and eloquence of diction, a careful
judgment and discrimination, which must give
the work a very high place in the permanent
literature of the nation.   It would be the highest
commendation to his work, to say that he has
done justice to his subject, yet, doubtless by this
well-written and skilfully compacted volume,
Mr. Macdonald has helped to fix and perpetuate
his own fame, and has worthily linked his name
with that of the immortal Punshon.

And yet, though I may be charged with something like presumption, I have to confess to a
feeling of disappointment with the volume.
There is a lack of warmth, a chill in the biography, which is something amazing and un-
looked for in the life of one who was indeed a
burning and a shining light, whose soul was
incandescent, whose whole being was intense,
and glowing with fervent heat.

Perhaps the writer's scholarly and critical habit of mind may account for the temperature of the narration, but it is a sore lack. I know not exactly what were Mr. Macdonald's personal relations to Dr. Punshon. I judge that they were close and intimate, if so, and it were his privilege to rejoice in the sunlight of his warm personality, then, he has, like the moon, reflected with consummate brilliance and beauty the light of the sun, but not its vivifying heat.

Again, one feels a certain inadequacy with which his life is represented in these pages. The real personality has to be read into it. The unwritten seems so much more than the written. But this brings up the query as to how far it is possible for a biography to gather up the sense of personality, and give it out to the reader. Another serious defect in this biography, it seems to me, is the undue prominence given to journal records of "sadness and depression." Dr. Punshon suffered at times from intense depression of spirits and various physical distresses. His sensitive nature felt the loss of personal friends and eminent ministers

in the wide circle of his acquaintance, he was
a mourner over many tombs; his very refine-
ment of temperament, and that great-hearted-
ness which gave him such a mighty force in
vital affairs, by a natural reaction made him
also at times a victim of nervous melancholy,
but he was not a man of sadness and gloom.
No one who knew him and companioned with
him, but remembers him as a man of sunshine
and cheer, of exuberant flow of spirits, and
possessing a nature which, though beaten upon
by constant storms of sorrow, had wonderful
powers of resiliency and recuperation.

These records reveal a side of life wholly unknown to multitudes, the private sorrows and
anxieties, the spiritual conflicts and inner distresses of one whose outward course was that
of unbroken and unclouded popularity. But
the extracts are too largely of this character,
and are therefore misleading. They give a
sombreness to the life; they make his piety
seem morbid and unhealthy, and not robust and
manly as it was. He had times of morbid retro-
spection, when he was delivered up to the

darkest fears and imaginings, but the joy of
the Lord was his strength, and he walked ex-
ultantly in the light of His salvation. He loved
life and would fain see many days; he spoke
of the rapture of living, and feared lest his love
of life were too strong. The notes taken from
his diary are in the minor key. The mournful
tones and semi-tones, the plaints of distress
overpower the *Jubilate Deo*—the genial, exultant, sunny characteristics, the records of joy-
ousness of soul, and delight in God.

There is one other distinctive mark set upon
this volume. The writer is a critic more than
a biographer, and never loses sight of this. He
is a sagacious, scholarly man, full of analytical
skill and high-toned discretion, and everything
must be judged with the utmost coolness, accuracy, and discrimination. He will not be
accused of adulation; he writes with great can-
dor and honesty, and an evident desire to place
the character and productions of Dr. Punshon
in a correct light before the world. While he
does not depreciate the endowments of his
friend, he yet uses the most moderate expres-

sions of admiration for his literary perform-
ances, and does not spare the faults and weak-
nesses of his style. In general, the criticisms
are so thoughtful and appreciative, so impartial
and discriminating, as to compel admiration,
yet at times the censure is so severe, the lack
of early education made so much of, and the
estimate so much in the direction of disparage-
ment that the reader begins to wonder whether
the biographer-critic is not, by the very severity
of his taste, somewhat disqualified to pronounce
upon the orator's best exertions, or to assign to
their true and exalted place those prodigious
orations whose energy and brilliance carried
everything before them.

Notwithstanding what we have here said, this
volume is a worthy memorial of him who held
so high a place in public estimation, and will
go down to remote posterity a blessing and living source of piety and inspiration to thousands
and tens of thousands. The purpose of the
present writer is to give to those who have not
been able to procure this large and well-written
biography, such extracts and selections, together

with correspondence and matter not previously published, as will enable them to follow the course of Dr. Punshon's life, and to appreciate the character of one of the noblest of "the men worth remembering."

William Morley Punshon, the only child of John and Elizabeth Punshon, was born at Doncaster, May 29th, 1824. His father was a consistent Christian and a hearty Methodist, and his mother, Elizabeth Morley, was a woman of simple devotion and tender love, the sister of the saintly Margaret Clough, who, as a missionary's wife on her way to Ceylon, makes this entry in her journal :

"Written at sea, Sunday, May 29th, 1825. This is my dear little nephew's birthday. May the God of his father generously condescend to take this tender infant into His peculiar care ; and, if spared, may he be an ornament to the Church of God."

Was ever yearning desire more fully realized ! Who could have dreamed that within that wee baby-thing were stored potencies so mighty as to move and thrill the hearts of millions in both hemispheres !

The biographer dwells upon the influences which wrought upon William Morley Punshon's child-life. His home, a godly household, with its tranquil round of Sunday and week-day services, prayer and class-meetings, with now and again a party of Christian friends. Such quiet and well-ordered homes are indeed among the chief sources of the strength of Methodism. At this shrine was lighted the flame of the future preacher's zeal; here he learned to love those doctrines and usages to which he was so steadfastly devoted through all his life. As a child, he gave signs of more than ordinary powers, and the writer expresses regret that in his eager, quick-budding springtime, the means of culture and discipline were not more abundantly available. His school-life began in Doncaster, and was over before he had completed his fourteenth year. His love of poetry showed itself very early, and when only eight years of age, he would commit to memory some favourite lines, and repeat them in a vigorous and spirited style.

While in the Grammar School, he and his

friend Ridgill, with two other boys, formed
themselves into a society called the *Quaternity*,
which had for its object the pursuit of adven-
tures. While at school, at Heanor, in Derby-
shire, the friendship between him and Gervase
Smith began, and through all changes those
early friendships remained unvarying and abid-
ing.

The passion of his boyhood was for poetry
and political oratory. He has often told me of
the enthusiasm he had for political life, what a
strange fascination the debates in Parliament
had over him, and that he could repeat entire
speeches of Peel and Palmerston, and that he
ran wild over the stirring lyrics and elaborate
addresses of Macaulay. His early ambition was
to obtain a seat in the House of Commons, and
enter the political arena. How these fair hopes
were destined to disappointment! Providence
was working out something higher and better
for him.

In June, 1838, his mother died. There had
existed between them the tenderest affection,
the most intimate companionship, and he was

heart-stricken with grief over his loss. The sense of loneliness, the despondency, and the sorrow, resulted in a state of deep mental depression, and he traced the beginning of his nervous melancholy and ill health to this sorrow over his mother's death. The author says, "Mrs. Punshon was buried under the shadow of the old church in Doncaster, near the entrance to the south transept. Henceforth it was sacred ground to her son. Thirty years after, his wife by his side, he knelt and kissed his mother's gravestone, and spoke with emotion of the great loss her death had been to him." His mother's death awakened in his soul spiritual longings, and he was under deep and strong conviction of sin. He had never received any marked or clear evidence of his acceptance with God, and he longed for faith in Christ as a personal Saviour, and for peace with God.

. The way of salvation was revealed to him, and there came that great vital, inward change which revolutionized his character and made him what he was. Concerning this spiritual event, which took place when he was a boy

about fourteen and a half years old, he wrote to
his aunt:—

"It was on the 29th of November, I had previously
been in great distress of mind, when, as I was walking
on the dock side, I was met by the Rev. S. R. Hall,
who urged upon me the necessity of immediate belief.
Then and there I was enabled to lay hold on my
Saviour, and peace immediately sprang up in my heart."
P. 22.

He at once joined the Methodist Society in
Hull, where he was now residing, and his religion took on a very practical and experimental
form.   He attended the prayer-meetings, class-
meetings, love-feasts, became a prayer-leader
and Sunday-school teacher.   The spirit of Methodism gave direction and character to his
growth in the Divine life, and the doctrines and
usages, the traditions and ministries of the
Church became a part of himself.

About this time his first attempts were made
at debating and public speaking, in a society
for mutual improvement, called the *Menticul-*
tural Society, which consisted of eight or ten
close friends and companions in religious life.
It is remarkable that every one of these young

men subsequently entered the ministry. He mentions in letters written at this time, that now and then this *Menticultural* had a Biblical night, Brother Smith taking a Greek Bible, Prof. Punshon a Latin, Bishop Lyth a Hebrew, and Dr. Locking a German, in order to mark variations in the text.

About this time too, thoughts of preaching took possession of his mind, and he began to have definite convictions about entering the ministry. On Sunday, August 2nd, 1840, at the age of sixteen, William Morley Punshon preached his first sermon. A letter to his cousin narrates the circumstances attending this memorable event.

"HULL, August 5th, 1840.

"On Sunday last, at 7 a.m., I went to our band, and we had a very profitable time. At ten o'clock I went to see them at the school, and about half-past ten J. Lyth came in, and he and I started for Ellerby, where he had to preach twice. Having only one sermon ready, the other was to be an extemporaneous effusion. We arrived; the congregation in the afternoon was twenty-four souls, and he preached his only sermon, from 'Behold the Lamb of God,' etc. In the evening we did not know what to do, so it was agreed that we should each

deliver an address, and then hold a prayer-meeting.
After having implored the presence and blessing of the
Holy Spirit, we both mounted the pulpit. It had been
arranged that I should speak for ten minutes, and then
he should finish.   I gave out, 'Come sinners to the
Gospel feast,' then prayed, then read the lesson—a long
chapter—then gave out, 'The great archangel's trump
shall sound,' and then announced my text, 'And as Paul
reasoned of righteousness, temperance, and judgment
to come, Felix trembled,' etc.   I got into the subject,
and, with the help of God, spoke for between half and
three-quarters of an hour, and left him nothing to do but
conclude." P. 29.

From that hour, the current of his life began
to set steadily toward the Christian ministry.
In December, 1840, his father died, and the lad's
orphanhood was complete.   But, he had the
precious realization that God was his Father,
and the germ of that life hid with Christ in
God was developing into flower and fruit.

He was now living in Sunderland with his
uncle, Mr. Panton, and had plenty of work upon
his hands in the way of preaching.   The note
authorizing him to preach preliminary to his becoming a recognized local preacher, was given
by the Rev. Thos. S. Squance, and he entered

with singleness of eye and glowing zeal upon the work of declaring the unsearchable riches of Christ. Our author has enlarged with great animation and remarkable beauty upon his spirit and labours as a local preacher.

"The interest which he felt in politics, though not extinct, was now altogether subordinate. A passion for preaching, to which his natural gifts and religious aspirations alike contributed, had become the master-passion of his soul. Along with the delight that attends the exercise of oratorical powers, there came a deeper insight into the great realities of sin and redemption, and a graver, more chastened estimate of the office and work of the minister of Christ. It was well, indeed, that misgivings, and conflicts, and inward humiliation were given in this precocious springtime, when, perhaps, the one thing to be feared was a too swift and easy blossoming. The difficulties involved in the preparation and delivery of sermons, which are in themselves a discipline for most young preachers, hardly existed for him. He sermonized with ease; divisions, paragraphs, sentences, took shape as fast as his flying pen could fix them. There was no laborious committing to memory—that was accomplished in the act of composing. What he wrote he could recall, page after page, with perfect accuracy and freedom; while his delivery, rapid, rushing, yet subtly modulated, charmed the ear and strangely

3

touched the emotions. These were great gifts—gifts
rather than acquirements. What many men by slow de-
grees, through continued effort, in some measure come
to possess, was his he knew not how. Little more than
a boy, he began to preach, and at once found himself
famous. The people flocked to hear him. The chapels
were crowded. He was pressed to preach at Doncaster,
and seventeen hundred people filled Priory Place Chapel.
Invitations poured in upon him from the towns and
villages near Sunderland, and from Hull. He entered
at once upon the honours and upon the perils of a
popular preacher. And surely none would lightly estimate those perils in the case of one so young as William
Morley Punshon, whose temperament—affectionate, im-
pressible, ever craving sympathy, and susceptible to pain
and pleasure at the hands of others—would naturally
expose him to all the dangers of the position. But the
safeguards were forthcoming. As has been said, they
consisted in part of the inner spiritual discipline by
which it pleased God to chasten him, and, in part at
least, the wholesome, practical work of the prayer-
meeting, the Sunday-school, the mission band, served to
keep him in touch with homely people and humble ways,
and maintain the balance of things as against the exciting influences of popular services and admiring crowds.
By a special grace of God his conscience had been
awakened to the evil of vanity, and to the presence of
something in himself that was either that, or the root

and beginning of it. He took the warning, and fought this enemy down to its lurking-places. The victory was given him with such completeness, that few ever knew of the danger, and of the way in which it had been over-come. On this defeated vice the opposing virtue was established with such happy mastery that, through his after career, of all the tributes he received from friends, and particularly from his brethren in the ministry, the most frequent was that which was rendered to his hu-mility. It was a common saying that nothing was more wonderful in Punshon than his modesty." Pp. 36-38.

Mr. Squance desired to propose young Pun-shon as a candidate for the ministry at the March Quarterly Meeting of 1843; but he had the keenest sense of the responsibility of the office, and wanted more time for prayer, self-examination and preparation. It was finally arranged that he should spend a few months with his uncle, Rev. B. Clough, then stationed at Woolwich, that he might aid him in his studies.

Before leaving Sunderland he published a volume of verse, entitled " Wild Flowers," and of these youthful productions the biographer says :—

" It is not necessary to submit them to serious criticism. They show, not so much direct poetical impressions, as the influence upon a warm and lively fancy of the poetry that he had read. Their chief interest at this distance is biographic. They illustrate some events in his history, and show the kind of topics that interested him, and furnished themes for his early efforts in verse. Perhaps the truest note of feeling is uttered in the poem entitled, 'Lines on the Anniversary of a Mother's Death.'" P. 40.

From boyhood he had devoured poetry with great eagerness; and, subtle in thought and feeling, of fine, delicate organization and poetical susceptibilities and tastes, "What marvel if he thus essayed to sing?" Mr. Macdonald adds—

"The writing of verse long continued to be a recreation, but, as his true calling grew upon him, and took completer possession of his life, it occupied an entirely subordinate position; and, while affording pleasure from time to time to himself and to his friends, never really came into competition with his more serious labours." P. 42.

In due time he was proposed as a candidate and accepted by vote of the Circuit Quarterly Meeting, thus passing "the first of the gates that guard the approach to the Methodist ministry."

In September, 1844, he entered the Theological Institution at Richmond, and threw himself heartily into his studies. But his college career came to an unexpected termination, owing to the reason that he had by mistake been entered as a missionary student, while himself and his friends preferred the home-work, and since there was no room for him amongst the home-students, he was taken from Richmond and placed on the list of reserves. The comment which the writer makes on this matter, is exceedingly judicious :—

"At this distance of time it may be allowed, without attributing blame to any one, to express regret that such a proceeding was possible in the case of a student of much promise and of unblemished character. Taken in connection with the short and often interrupted course of his early education, it was peculiarly unfortunate that just as he was falling in with the conditions of college-life and study, the order of things should be once more dislocated, and he himself transferred from the lecture-room and library to the duties and responsibilities of the ministry. It may, perhaps, be urged, not without plausibility, that the same Providence that had cast him to such an extent, even as a boy, upon his own mental instincts and appetites, was once again setting aside arrangements which, for most men immeasurably the best, were not the best for him." P. 48.

I make this quotation all the more readily, as it strikes me that the scholarly biographer has made altogether too much of what he calls his lack of "early education." True, he had not a university training; but he had all the finish which literary acquirements could bestow. In boyhood he learned quickly and mastered fully the ground he had traversed. His memory was retentive, and he laid a good foundation on which to build up knowledge. He was an intense worker, and if not a profound and finished scholar, he had that ripeness of culture which gave him an ascendancy over the most educated minds. His classical allusions were most frequent, and the most cultured listened to him with the highest delight. He possessed a large amount of multifarious knowledge, and he was versed in all the phases of modern thought. It is a question whether a university career could have made him more effective than he **was,** and it is doing him scant justice to dwell upon his need of progressive, well - ordered study. Robert Hall says of the learned Keppis, "He might be a very clever man by nature, for aught I know, but he laid so many books upon his head that his brains could not move."

We have to bear in mind that Dr. Punshon's career was thrust upon him by a Providence, which he could not disregard, to be a preacher rather than a scholar and a theologian. Had he chosen the scholar's desk, he might have been as renowned for the depth and versatility of his attainments, as for his popular and effective eloquence. He was impelled by circumstances into the work, and like Spurgeon, the preacher of the age, he proved himself, without college preparation, a master workman.

He was now at the disposal of the President for supplying any vacancy, and was sent to Marden, in Kent, where a secession had taken place from the parish church, on account of " Puseyite " practices, and a request presented that a Methodist preacher might be sent to them. A delicate post, indeed, for one with so little ministerial capital to fill, and here he began his pastoral work. The biographer says:—

"To the delight of preaching was now added the interest of pastoral work. He gave his afternoons to visiting, and found that a minister has other means of usefulness to the souls of his people than those belonging to the pulpit. And what was good for them was no less serviceable for him. No man needs the discipline of pastoral work more than the popular preacher. Tendencies to the unreal, the artificial, the high-flying, are best checked and qualified by intercourse with the sick and sorrowful, by experience of practical ministering amid the varied conditions of actual every day life. The months spent at Marden were happy and useful ones. His preaching attracted large congregations. By some of his 'parishoners,' as he called them, he was strongly urged to seek orders in the Church of England, with the assurance that a church should be built for him. But neither then nor at any later period did he falter for a moment in his allegiance to Methodism. It cost him no effort to refuse the kind proposal. He set himself rather, as he had playfully said, 'to make some Methodists.' A society was organized, a chapel built, and when the time came for him to leave the Kentish village where he had served his short apprenticeship to the ministry, a probation before the probation which had its formal beginning at the Conference of 1845, he could look back

with thankfulness on good work done, and useful lessons
learnt.

"In the minutes of the Conference of 1845, the name
of W. M. Punshon occurs for the first time. It stands
under the head of 'Preachers now received on trial,'
together with the names of Thomas McCullagh, George
Mather, and Ebenezer Jenkins, almost the only survivors
of the men of that year. Although his exceptional
pulpit popularity was now becoming widely known, he
was not appointed to one of the more important or
exacting circuits. There is, indeed, something amounting almost to a tradition in Methodism, that distinguished men spend the earlier years of their ministry
in obscure places. After a while the great centres claim
their services, and afford them more adequate sphere
for their powers ; but scores of instances might be ad-
duced to show that 'country circuits' have been the
training-ground of the men who have afterwards risen
to honour and authority."

He started from the lowest round of the lad-
der, on one of the worst circuits in all Methodism, and among the roughest elements, he
began that career which excited so profound,
and extended, and prolonged a sensation in the
public mind. Full of fervour and enthusiasm,
this plain, unassuming young man girded him-

self for his work, and laboured with all his
heart among the country people, and his eloquence evinced itself as the flame and impetus
of a mighty genius.   The author quotes from
the Rev. Thos. McCullagh, who had the happiness to hear Mr. Punshon's first missionary
speech delivered at Harrington, a quaint little
seaport, on the Whitehaven Circuit:—

"I was prepared," says Mr. McCullagh, "for something good, as accounts reached Workington almost
daily of the wonderful young preacher who had come to
Whitehaven.   But when I heard for myself, I found that
the half had not been told me.   The rush of brilliant
thoughts and burning words, the perfect whirlwind of
eloquence, almost took away my breath.   I do not know
that I was more enraptured with his speeches at Exeter
Hall in after years, than with that first platform effort
during the first weeks of his ministry.   We used to call
it his 'Excitement speech,' as he dwelt in it upon the
excitements of novelty, opposition, and success, by
which the missionary enterprise had been supported in
turns, until, at last, it came to rest upon principle."

In his first platform address, his maiden effort,
he achieved that marked success which constituted him a king among platform speakers.   At

once this brilliant young man became a heroic, fiery advocate of missions—not a missionary, but a creator of missions and missionaries, planting in men's hearts seeds of missionary effort that were to spring up in ever-widening harvests to the end of time. Whoever has heard him at his best, in the zenith of his popularity and power, can imagine the utter bewilderment of wonder, which this beginning of surprises must have occasioned to those who were present at his first missionary speech.

Mr. McCullagh goes on to say, "In the May of 1846, he attended his first District Meeting, at Carlisle. He and I lodged together at a village two miles from the city, and as we had to preach on successive mornings at five o'clock, an early start was necessary. We arranged between us that he was to remain awake all night in order to waken me, as I had to preach the first morning. I promised to do the same for him the next night ; but, alas, the willing spirit was overmatched by the weak flesh, and the watchman overslept himself. Finding ourselves considerably behind time, in order to recover some of it we ran the whole of the two miles. Arrived at the chapel, we found the Rev. Samuel Rowe giving out a hymn from his pew. Mr. Punshon entered the pulpit, and preached a remarkably beautiful and eloquent sermon. After the service I breakfasted with some of the ministers at the house of Mr. James. The preacher of the morning not being present, much of the conversation at the breakfast-table turned on the sermon, wonderful from any one, but especially from a probationer in his first year."

That five o'clock sermon, preceded by the two miles run, preached in the old border city, made such an impression upon those who heard it, that the Carlisle Quarterly Meeting at once invited him to become their pastor on the completion of his second year at Whitehaven. To this circuit he was appointed in 1847. The cause was low, and rent by divisions; but during the two years spent in the staid cathedral city, he filled the half-empty chapels with eager and delighted hearers.

II.

I HAVE a vivid remembrance that when on the old Griffintown Circuit, Montreal, I laboured as a young man with Rev. Dr. Douglas, among my choicest friends were the late Mr. and Mrs. Daniel Hadley. Mrs. Hadley was an English woman of unusual piety and intelligence, and was a young lady living in Carlisle during Mr. Punshon's pastorate there; and I have listened for hours to her descriptions of his appearance and surpassing popularity. She described him as a young man with round boyish face; his auburn hair, thick and curly; his eyes, keen and piercing; his figure, muscular, but thin; and his appearance and manner, most refined and gentleman-like. He would enter the pulpit with modest, downcast look, and read the hymn in such a way as to arrest the attention of everyone. His voice, she described as being husky at the start, but always clear and ringing to the close. She dwelt upon his beautiful enunciation and the emphasis he would give every now and then to certain words; and the sermons she described as gardens of loveliness, filled with flowers of every variety of beauty, and charm of shape, and colour and perfume. His influence over the young people she described as very great; his genial, sunny, yet dignified ways, drawing all around him, and getting them to see new blessedness and joy in religious things. Mr. Macdonald, in one of the finest pieces of description in the book, pictures the crowded congregations in the old Fisher St. Chapel, all under the spell of his pulpit powers:—

"The recognized classifications of orthodox and heterodox, Church-people and Nonconformists, professional men and tradespeople, were confounded in this new order of things. Persons found themselves side by side in the Methodist chapel who had never been in one before, who had never met one another there or elsewhere. Anglican clergymen, Dissenting ministers, Roman Catholics and Quakers, gentlefolks from the city, and squires from the country, lawyers and doctors, shopkeepers, farmers, and labourers, with here and there an itinerant actor—all sorts and conditions of men to be found in or near the old border capital, flocked to hear the young preacher, and to be excited, subdued, moved by a pulpit oratory unlike anything they had ever heard.

" It was not subtlety or originality of thought, or novelty of doctrine, that drew the crowds and held them in breathless, and often painful, suspense. In respect of doctrine it was Methodist preaching as generally understood, and there was little sign of new or deeper insight into familiar truth; but there was a glow, a sweep, an exultant rush of quick-following sentences, exuberant in style—too much so, a critic might say,—that culminated now and then in passages of overwhelming declamation, or sank to a pathos that brought tears to unaccustomed eyes. His whole soul was in his work. The ornate musical sentences, full of harmonious delights for the ear, were no mere literary devices ; they were his natural modes of expression, raised and quickened by the emotions of the preacher's heart. His voice, often harsh and husky at first, would clear and strengthen as he proceeded, revealing unexpected range and power of modulation. His constrained, uneasy attitude grew free and graceful ; he stood erect, the left arm held behind him, with his right hand, instinct with nervous life, he seemed to grasp his audience, to summon and dismiss arguments, to cut his way through difficulties, until, with uplifted face, radiant with spiritual light, both hands were outstretched in impassioned climax, or raised as in contemplation of some glory seen from afar." Pp. 63-64.

At the Manchester Conference of 1849, he was ordained, the charge being delivered by Rev. Dr. Newton, and appointed to Newcastle-upon-Tyne. With his ordination vows fresh upon him, he took upon him the vows of matrimony, for immediately after Conference he was married to Miss Maria Vickers, of Gateshead, an amiable, intelligent and devoted young lady, the child of Christian parents, and well-fitted by character, culture and personal experience of Divine grace, to be a true help-meet to her husband. Sustained by a firm trust in God, and by the sympathy of his true-hearted young wife, he went to his new and difficult appointment. The "agitation" in connection with the " fly-sheets" and the expulsion of Revs. Everett, Dunn and Griffith, greatly disturbed his Tyneside Circuit of sixteen hundred members; but the tide of his mighty pulpit popularity swept everything before it. The sphere of his labours was continually widening, and all the border counties were roused, dazzled and taken captive by this young Apollos, so eloquent and mighty in the Scriptures.

Amid the ever-broadening circle of life and labours the biographer gives, what is all too rare in the volume, some glimpses of his happy home-life. His domestic affections were the strongest; he loved home, and in the midst of unremitted exertions his heart turned home- ward, as the centre of his happiness, and in his family life he found a joy amounting to rapture. In December, 1850, Fanny Morley was born, and before he left Newcastle, John William. How his father-heart rejoiced over these treas- ures, and how the life went out of him when they were taken away.

From Newcastle he was removed to Sheffield, where his pulpit and platform engagements multiplied, and he began to feel the strain of these ever-increasing labours. Here he received —a minister of but seven years' standing—an invitation from the Missionary Committee, in London, to preach and speak at the May anni- versary. His rising reputation had made it necessary that he should be heard at the head-

4

quarters of the connexion. Of this London work, he wrote to a friend, " I exceedingly fear and quake."

ST. PAUL'S CATHEDRAL, LONDON.

What the biographer says of his first appear-

ance at Exeter Hall, will be read with deep
interest :—

"The words of the young and eloquent speaker pro-

ST. PAUL'S CATHEDRAL (INTERIOR).

duced a great impression. It was felt that another man
had arisen to stand among the foremost defenders and

advocates of Christian Missions. And from that hour
it was so. He had taken possession of Exeter Hall, to
retain it to his life's end. Of all who have trodden its
historic platform none have moved the eager thousands
that pack within its walls with completer mastery than
he. The promise of this was discerned by some, at
least, of those who heard his first speech. But in looking back upon that meeting an interest attaches to it
which time only could bring to light. It was Robert
Newton's last appearance at the anniversary of the
Wesleyan Missionary Society, and Morley Punshon's
first. For the first and last time they stood together in
the cause with which their names must always be linked.
The elder handed the torch to the younger and passed
away. That May morning, in 1853, divides the earlier
from the later period of missionary advocacy. The
name of Robert Newton may stand for the one, the
name of Morley Punshon for the other." P. 89.

Mr. Punshon himself, writing about the meeting to his intimate friend, Rev. Thos. McCullagh,
says:—

"The most gratifying thing to me was, not the
crowded congregations on Sabbath, nor the reception
at the meeting, though it was warm, but that after the
meeting, the old doctor—the great lion—the veritable
Jabez Bunting, hobbled across the committee-room for
the express purpose of shaking hands with me, and

telling me that it gave him pleasure to see and hear me there." P. 89.

And he adds—

"Fancy the change from Exeter Hall to Peasenhall, down in the wilds of Suffolk, beyond the limits of the twopenny post, where I began the missionary sermon with *four* people, and the collection at the meeting was five-and-twenty shillings !"

His visit to London brought him an invitation to lecture for the Young Men's Christian Association, at Exeter Hall, and the response to this summons proved to be one of the most important events in his entire career.

I distinctly remember Dr. Punshon telling me how he came to deliver his first lecture, and to adopt his sermonlike style of lectures. The Exeter Hall lectures formed one of the agencies of the Young Men's Christian Association for promoting the spiritual and mental improvement of the young men of the metropolis. Mr. W. Edwyn Shipton, the Secretary, had heard him preach his sermon on Elijah, and struck with his power to portray character, his chaste and classical diction, his captivating and impressive delivery, he at once suggested to him that he transform the sermon into a lecture for young men, giving it a little wider range and more elastic mode of treatment. He faltered and hesitated, but at length consented and began to rearrange his matter, and elaborate his discourse under the title of "The Prophet of Horeb." Many a time he repented his rash promise, and was on the eve of giving up the effort. He thought it presumption to undertake to make his disguised sermon interesting and profitable to that lecture-audience of two or three thousand. But the oration was completed, and at the time announced, delivered, and let the author relate, in his own inimitable way, Mr. Punshon's first triumph as a lecturer:—

"On the 17th of January, 1854, he delivered his lecture on 'The Prophet of Horeb,' in Exeter Hall, to nearly three thousand people. He spoke for two hours with perfect command of himself, his subject, and his audience. 'Towards the close,' says one who was present, 'There was the stillness and solemnity of death, you might have heard a feather fall in that vast assembly;

and when the last sentence had fallen from his lips,
the whole audience rose *en masse* and cheered till it
could cheer no more.'" Pp. 91-92.

His ministry in Sheffield terminated at the
Conference of 1855, and was in every way
a successful one. Concerning it, he himself
writes :—

"My course in Sheffield has been a very happy one.
The circuit was low, and it has been raised by the blessing of God upon our labours. We have added about
three hundred members in the course of the last year.
For twelve months we have scarcely had a Sabbath
evening without witnessing conversions. Three of us
hold prayer-meetings after every service, save, of course,
on sacramental occasions, and the good resulting from
this old-fashioned plan is inestimable. I have had
agreeable colleagues." P. 92.

It is refreshing to think of his returning from
anniversary services, missionary meetings and
crowded lecture halls ; from a ministry through
the connexion at large, to meet classes, hold
prayer-meetings, preach and labour for the salvation of souls. It was his chiefest delight to
bring sinners to God ; and brilliant preacher

though he was, while thousands went away
from his sermon to admire, not a few went
away to repent and seek after God. He has
often told me, with the tears in his eyes, that
no joy in his ministry was equal to the joy that
was given him in the conversion of souls. He
hungered for this. No one who knew anything
of his inner life could doubt the depth and
genuineness of his devotion to God, or that he
used his exceptional popularity in the service
of his Master, and for the highest good of men.
He was deprived of all leisure and retirement,
he had to live in public and amid constant
excitements. He had always to meet high-
pitched expectation, and was keyed up to the
loftiest efforts, yet his piety was deep and fervent, and he constantly longed for the heart of
purity, and the tongue of fire. I have travelled
with him thousands of miles on the swift rail,
the steamer, the stage-coach, yet everywhere
he cultivated the spirit of prayer and quiet
waiting upon God, and was in the regular habit
of reading daily some book of devotion. Amid
the perils of popularity his spiritual life was

supported, and prayer was his constant resource.
Mr. Macdonald has well put the dangers of the
popular preacher :—

"Interpreting God's will by all the indications of it
that are within our reach, we conclude that it was by
the will of God that William Morley Punshon came to
be the most itinerant member of the itinerant ministry
to which he belonged.

"But a price has to be paid for this. The price is,
in part, the toil of constant travelling, with absence from
home and family, and, in part, a certain peril to the
inner life, deprived of quiet resting-places, and given
over to hurry and excitement. What time is there for
patient waiting upon truth, for meditation, for 'the harvest of a quiet eye,' and of a mind at leisure? What
discipline is to preserve the simplicity of one who is
followed by eager, expectant crowds? How is humility
to live in an atmosphere shaken by the frequent applause of multitudes? When all men speak well of
him, can he do other than think well of himself? And
after crowded services, breathless congregations, and
admiration and homage of many kinds, how will he be
disposed for humble exercises of prayer and self-examination, for ministering to the sick and sorrowful, and
showing piety at home?

"Mr. Punshon's journal reveals his jealousy over his
own soul. It shows him humbled, depressed, sorrowful,

even in the days of his most abundant popularity. He was never content to live upon the applause, so lavishly bestowed upon him, and at times it only helped to distress him.   There was a region of his spiritual life from which both world and Church were shut out, where not a breath of the praise of men was allowed to enter, where he knelt perpetually—humble, penitent, prayerful—at the feet of Jesus." P. 105.

From Sheffield Mr. Punshon removed to Leeds, another stronghold of Yorkshire Methodism, where, besides performing the duties of his own circuit, he went on with his itinerant ministry through the Connexion at large, visiting nearly one hundred different towns each year, preaching and lecturing.   Here Mrs. Punshon's health began to decline, and thenceforth she became the loved object of untold solicitude and anxiety to her husband.

At the Conference of 1858, Mr. Punshon, at the age of thirty-four, was called to populous London, Hinde Street Circuit, and Bayswater was chosen as a suitable place of residence for his invalid wife.   The claims upon him now became almost innumerable; but while the people flocked to hear him and packed the largest buildings, the heart of the rarely-gifted preacher was wrung with sorrow and the bitterness of death. His wife's mother died under his roof in October, 1859, and one dreary afternoon in November of the same year, the beloved wife of his youth "languished into life." "Going, going to glory," were her last words.

In the midst of his overwhelming sorrow he writes, "I have consecrated myself afresh to the great work to which God has called me. My darling children are very interesting and affectionate. God gives me comfort in them amid my grief and trouble." Out of this sevenfold heated furnace he emerged into a more tender, heart-searching and successful ministry, for the prophet who consoles others must himself be "a man of sorrows and acquainted with grief."

While at Bayswater, Mr. Punshon set himself to raise by his lecture on "The Huguenots," the sum of one thousand pounds for the old chapel at Spitalfields. The amount was raised in six months, but what an excessive bodily and mental tension this labour of love cost him no one can tell. His second term in the Metropolis was spent at Islington, where his popularity and influence still extended, and honours and successes crowded thick upon him. Here he commenced the arduous task of raising by lectures and other means £10,000 to give grants to aid in the erection of chapels in places of summer resort. The proceeds of his lectures on "Daniel in Babylon," " Macaulay," " Wesley and his Times," and " Wilberforce," were devoted to his watering-places fund. Not only did this freely-assumed burden and responsibility draw lavishly upon his great strength, but there were other special claims making demands at the same time upon one of such abounding popularity, as appeals on behalf of the distressed in Lancashire, arising out of the " Cotton Famine ;" the Jubilee Missionary movement of 1863, and the Metropolitan Chapel Building Fund of 1865.

The stress of incessant work was too great. His health and spirits began to give way; he was the victim of a strange nervous affection, which compelled him to desist from lecturing for nearly two years, and to give up all week-

day engagements. He sought rest and change
in travel on the continent, accompanied by his
faithful friend, Rev. Gervase Smith. The extracts from this journal of travel form one of
the most attractive portions of the biography.
Few men enjoyed travel more than he, and with
what zest and brilliant imagery he has described
the historic places visited; " the beauty and
chivalry" of Brussels, the field of Waterloo,
Strasburg and Lucerne with Rigi and Pilatus,
the Staubbach Falls, Berne and Lausanne, Lake
Maggiore, and Milan with its famous Duomo
and Church of St. Ambrose. How he loved
that marble wilderness, Milan's Cathedral. On
his last homeward journey, stricken with his
fatal illness, as we reached Turin and rested
there for three days, he insisted that I should
go on to Milan and see that " poem in stone,"
as well as visit the old church in which St.
Ambrose ministered and where Augustine heard
the words of Life.

He endeavoured also to see all sides of foreign
questions, enter into continental life, politics and
religion. He records his impressions of the

work of Christian missions in Europe as far as they passed under his keen eye, and returns from a journey of 3,000 miles, " having seen nineteen lakes, sixty-five rivers, fifty-two towns of more than 10,000 inhabitants, and crossed both Alps and Appenines." The enumeration is characteristic of the man.

On his return to Clifton he was able to resume in part his circuit duties, but was obliged to "go softly." Next year he made another journey to Italy, the route chosen being by way of Genoa, Pisa and the Riviera. In pleasant journeyings with loved companions, amid the beauties of nature and art, his health and spirits rapidly improved, he was recovering something of his old buoyancy and vigour.

About this time he wrote to Ridgill, the friend of his boyhood, " Do you ever essay poetry now ? I am foolish enough to meditate another volume, a sort of Methodist Christian Year. Whether it will ever appear time only can decide. The muse is capricious and wilful, and chooses the times of her visits and inspirations." Partly as a solace and a recreation, and

partly as a service to Christ, he prepared his
quiet meditations in verse for the Sundays of
a year; and in 1867 published "Sabbath
Chimes," the "offering of a year's enforced
pause amid the activities of a busy ministry."
The volume in its general method and spirit
is an imitation of Keble's "Christian Year," and
of it Mr. Macdonald says :—

"His 'Sabbath Chimes' was not unworthy of him; it
did not injure the reputation which he had secured by
labours of another kind; it gave pleasure, and ministered
to the devotion of many; it contains many a strong,
and many a soothing stanza; it is free from the morbid,
the sickly, the superstitious; its doctrine is scriptural,
its spirit reverent towards God, sympathetic towards
man; it contributed a strain or two to the permanent
enrichment of spiritual song; but, if it be asked, twenty
years after its publication, whether the writer derives
reputation from his book, or the book from its writer,
there can be no doubt as to the answer that must be
given. In other words, Mr. Punshon was, first and last,
a preacher, and his achievements in other directions,
including that of poetry, remain unmistakably subordinate." P. 263.

He had a deep, rich nature, a fine and fertile

imagination, an intuitive perception of the beautiful in thought and phrase; he possessed "the vision and faculty divine"; in short, all the susceptibilities and tastes of the poet; but his powers had not been concentrated upon poetry as an art, and his life had been too busy for great literary industry and the highest style of authorship. The completion of this volume of verse may have given him something of the feelings experienced by the great Wizard of the North, Sir Walter Scott, when he wrote the publisher on the last proof-sheet of his immortal work "Rob Roy":—

> "With very great joy
> I send you Roy.
> 'Twas a tough job,
> But we're done with Rob."

The "Chimes," however, will ring out their sacred peals on the Sabbath air for generations yet to come, and kindle the devotional life of thousands of the saints of God.

Mr. Punshon began once more to resume public work, and to the great delight of the entire Connexion reappeared upon the platform

of Exeter Hall at the May missionary meeting. In June he accompanied the Rev. William
Arthur to Belfast to attend the Irish Conference, and completed his undertaking on behalf
of the Watering Places Chapel Fund by raising
the magnificent sum of £10,697. By this noble
and self-imposed effort was secured the erection
of twenty-four new chapels in watering places,
and the enlargement and improvement of a
dozen more. Nearly eleven thousand sittings
were added to the church accommodation of
Methodism, while the sum raised through his
labours was the means of calling forth from
local efforts no less an amount than £62,727.
It may be said that this movement constituted
" a new departure " in Wesleyan chapel building
in England. These chapels, almost without exception, are elegant specimens of architecture,
and a permanent adornment of these charming
sea-side resorts.

During the year 1867 came the request from
the Conference of the Wesleyan Methodist
Church in Canada to the Parent Conference for
" the appointment of Rev. Wm. Morley Punshon

5

as its next President, and that he be permitted
to travel through the Connexion the current
year." The Conference acceded to the request,
and made the desired appointment. Mr. Punshon was further, by an almost unanimous vote,
appointed Representative of the British Conference to the General Conference of the Methodist Episcopal Church in the United States, to
be held in Chicago in the following May. His
ministry at Clifton closed in August, 1867, and
the months intervening between this time and
the following April, when he was to find " a
vocation and a home beyond the sea," were spent
in travel on the Continent, and in preaching
and lecturing in various parts of the country.

His last public engagement was a lecture in
Exeter Hall, on " Florence and its Memories."
Two hours before the appointed time the ap-
proaches to the doors were crowded, and at the
close of the lecture the immense audience, who
had been raised to the highest point of enthusiasm by his glowing and impassioned periods,
sprang to their feet, waved their hats and handkerchiefs, and by the most tumultuous applause,

again and again renewed, testified their delight, and conveyed their good wishes for his future.

The biographer seeks to reach the secret of Mr. Punshon's oratorical greatness, and to analyse the elements of his power. The learned Professor is inclined to follow the bent of his own genius, which is critical and philosophical, rather than sink his own idiosyncrasies and individuality in a faithful portraiture of his subject, leaving his sermons and lectures to take their own settled place in the public estimation.

The biographer is an admirable critic, but we cannot help thinking that in this instance he has unduly magnified his office. W. P. Frith, R.A., in his charming "Autobiography and Reminiscences," advises all artists, young and old, never to read art criticisms, for nothing is to be learned from them, and much undeserved pain is often inflicted. I suspect that similar objections lie against literary criticisms. True, there is here the utmost kindliness displayed by the critic; he would "hint the fault and hesitate dislike," always in the kindest spirit; yet one has to confess now and then to a groan of impatience over the biographer's performance in this direction.

It is open to question whether, with all the many-sidedness of the writer's views and feelings, he has not, in his very qualified estimate of Dr. Punshon's lectures, overlooked the fact that the orator speaks, and must speak, for present and immediate effect, for, except in the present, what good can speaking do. He read, and thought, and prepared his discourses with his great audiences before his mental vision, so that his clear, and powerful, and brilliant eloquence is not to be measured after the standard of the writer who carefully prepares an elaborate treatise for the scholarly reader. Nor should it be forgotten that these productions were the outpourings of a man of great power and thought, but of one whose life was so eager, and hurried, and public, that he was incessantly going from place to place, and had little time for profound and consecutive study.

The blemishes and imperfections noted in the lectures on "Bunyan," and on "Science and

Literature in relation to Religion," are not to be wondered at, for they were produced in his earlier years; yet for even these efforts the public had an admiration that scarcely stopped short of worship, and it is almost impossible to convey to the present generation the intense delight with which his thrilling and dazzling orations were received. Mr. Macdonald pays a high compliment to his ministerial fidelity when he says of his lectures: "They were but sermons carried from the pulpit to the platform, more broadly handled, and set forth with greater freedom of illustration and wealth of language."

On April 14, 1868, Mr. Punshon quitted the shores of much loved England for the New World. The record of his life and work on this continent is presented in five chapters, written by his son-in-law, Professor Reynar. With excellent judgment Professor Reynar allows Dr. Punshon to tell his own story in delightful letters and extracts from his journal, with valuable additions here and there, and rare glimpses into the heart and life of the grandly

gifted man. His first official duty was to convey to the General Conference at Chicago the
fraternal greetings of the British Conference.
I had the privilege of hearing his memorable
address. I had stood in the gallery of the Conference Church, wedged in among hundreds, for
more than an hour before the time announced
for the representatives to be introduced. The
great British orator was greeted with thunders
of applause. In a few crisp sentences he won
his hearers, and then, for an hour, he stirred
their pulses and their sensibilities, and swayed
them at will by his magnetic utterance and
the spell of his speech. The breathless attention, the rapturous applause of that great audience, I can never forget, and the effect of his
address was simply indescribable.

On Sabbath afternoon he preached in the
Opera House—and long before the hour announced the crowds swayed up and down before
the entrances. When the doors were opened
there was one rush up the broad staircases into
the spacious auditorium, until every inch of
standing room was occupied. The sermon was

founded upon Hebrews 12th chapter, 22–24 verses: "But ye are come unto Mount Zion," etc. The immense congregation was held spell-bound as he rose from climax to climax, pressing home upon the heart and the conscience the great truths of the Gospel, while the closing appeals of the earnest ambassador for Christ were uttered with an eloquence that defies description.

His first Canadian Conference was held in Kingston, June, 1868. My ministerial brethren of that time will remember how high were our expectations, and how fully they were met. Some of the men of the platform had fears lest his executive and administrative ability might not stand the test, but he showed a surprising mastery of details, and conducted the business of the Conference with an impartiality and despatch that delighted all. The Conference sermon is remembered as one of the most tender, spiritual and inspiring that ever fell from his lips, and the glow of language, the beauty of illustration, were merged in a spiritual intensity and unction in delivery that were even rare to him.

He secured a house in Toronto, owned by the late Mr. Robert Walker, and in August, his family having arrived, he writes: "Thank God they are here safe, and our four months' exile is over at last."

On the 15th of the same month he was united in marriage to Fanny Vickers, Rev. Dr. Ryerson performing the marriage ceremony.

Miss Vickers was the sister of his deceased wife, and had for ten years filled a mother's place to his four children—the only mother whom two had ever known. He loved her with a true devotion, but the English law declared marriage with a deceased wife's sister illegal. He would have submitted to that law, iniquitous and oppressive though he believed it to be, and treated the good and pure woman, whose faithful ministry had made his house a home, as his own sister. But this would not satisfy some, who insisted that he must either remove her from his home or marry another. After much and prayerful consideration of the subject, he deemed it his duty to marry her, even though it involved such great sacrifices as expatriation, the breaking up of old friend-

ships, the imputation of unworthy motives, and
even the imperilling of his usefulness. In
Canada there were not these legal objections,
and when the request came from the Canadian
Methodist Church to become their President
and dwell amongst them, the way seemed pro-
videntially opened to discharge the solemn duty
which rose up before him. At the bidding of
honour and affection, though he had to sacrifice
position and influence in the British Conference,
he went forth to found a home in the New
World, strong in the assurance that he was
doing right. And who that has ever dwelt in
the light and warmth of that charming home
could for a moment have a shadow of misgiv-
ing that he had not been led of the Lord, whose
guidance he continually invoked. Though admired and applauded everywhere, yet his great
heart hungered for domestic affection, and the
deep, rare blessedness of a happy home. Never
man more needed such a refuge for his heart;
and Mrs. Punshon possessed the beauty, the
charms, the sympathetic sweetness, the tenderness and kindness which will never cease to be
more dear to man than any amount of intel-

lect. She made his home a new centre of pleasant Christian society and life, and though indisposed to put her own personality forward, she yet won her gentle way, by a thousand quiet ministries, into the hearts of the people.

Established in Canada, he threw all his great energy and enthusiasm into the onward movements of the Church. Of large catholic sympathy and spirit, he yet felt that the Church of his choice should take her place, the peer of all, and he gave his matchless gifts to the advocacy of her educational, missionary and evangelizing work. Re-elected again and again, by virtually unanimous votes, to the Presidency of the Conference, his office was really episcopal, and his diocese was 1,500 miles in length, two or three hundred in width, with a population of three millions. On his re-election in 1869, he expressed his thankfulness that in a new climate, and through the changes of seasons and the perils of travel, he had been preserved in health and safety, and been privileged to conduct during the year *one hundred and seventy* public services, travelling, to render them, *sixteen thousand miles.* In every service he gave his best; he knew not how to spare himself, and how little the multitudes who witnessed his public appearances knew with what fears and painful apprehensions he appeared before them, or with what distress and nervous exhaustion the effort would be followed. Who that heard them can ever forget those addresses which he gave in the old Richmond Street Church to the people on their duties to the ministry, and to the ministers on their duties to the people? The excitement and the strain were too much. I was honoured with being a guest in his home at the time, and on Sabbath, after the service, he had an attack very similar to that which terminated his life. How different the spectacle of the preacher in the pulpit, flaming in the height of his brilliance, rising from climax to climax, swaying the multitude with over-mastering emotion; from the man approaching his work in tremor of body and agony of spirit, with nervous apprehensions of fainting and dying then and there, or when the extraordinary excitement was over, in bodily suffering and nervous exhaustion, even to faintness.

III.

AT the Conference of 1870, Dr. Punshon was visited by his life-long friend, Rev. Gervase Smith. His coming was to the President as cold water to the thirsty soul. How nervous he was over his friend's first appearance at the Conference, and how anxious that he should be received with befitting welcome. The reception was all that could be desired, and when the brethren gave themselves up to the spell of that eloquent, enthusiastic and most lovable man, his delight was unbounded. And what days those were in his own home, when the Conference sessions were over; the glee, the playful humour, the brilliant strokes of wit and repartee, the episodes and stories of the past, the sparkling and delightful conversation, the tender and true affection; the two great and gifted divines were

like boys together. What a change when I saw
the two friends together at Tranby, both broken
down in health and spirits, but loving each other
as of old. It was their last meeting on earth.
But a short time intervened between the departure of the two, so that "in their deaths they
were not divided."

The three departments of Church work to
which Dr. Punshon's best exertions were given
were the increased endowment of Victoria University, the Missionary work, and Church building extension. When the annual grant from
the Legislature was suddenly withdrawn in
1868, Mr. Punshon threw himself with great
earnestness into the movement for additional
College support, and in a short time endowments
were received which more than made up for the
loss of the grants from the Provincial treasury.
Prof. Reynar says:

"Victoria University is also indebted to Mr. Punshon
for his interest in the establishment of a theological
faculty, the first chair of which was endowed by the late
Edward Jackson, of Hamilton. His advocacy was also
given to the establishment, in the city of Montreal, of the

Wesleyan Theological College, to be affiliated to Victoria
. University." P. 335.

While greatly interested in our Domestic Mission work, and our French Canadian and Indian
Missions, he thought it was high time that Canadian Methodism was represented in the foreign
field, and the establishment of our Mission to
Japan was due to his advocacy and exertions,
coupled with those of a few of our own far-seeing
and zealous laymen and ministers. His last
official act was in a valedictory given to our
noble missionaries, Revs. George Cochran and
Davidson McDonald, who were starting for the
sunrise kingdom.

Another movement in which he took a prominent part was Methodist Union.

The Canadian biographer well says:

" In the readjustment of relations with the parent
Church in England it was of great advantage that one so
familiar with English Methodism and so influential in her
councils should be at the head of the Canadian Church.
It was not till the year 1874, the year after Mr. Punshon's
departure from Canada, that the first union took effect,
but he was actively concerned in the previous negotiations

which led to that union. The union of 1874 was of the Wesleyan Methodist Conference of Canada, the Wesleyan New Connexion Conference, and the Wesleyan Conference of Eastern British America. This was followed in 1883 by a further union of the Methodist Church of Canada, the Methodist Episcopal Church of Canada, the Bible Christian Church, and the Primitive Methodist Church. Thus was founded the present Canadian Methodist Church, into which all the Methodists of British America are gathered in one national Methodist Church of ten Conferences, 1,628 ministers, and a spiritual charge of some 800,000 souls, the largest Protestant Church in the Dominion." Pp. 331-32.

An impulse was also given to church building; and in cities, towns and rural places, beautiful churches were reared and consecrated to God's worship, and multitudes were drawn to the dedicatory services to hear the great orator. Says the writer : " The chief monument of the church extension and improvement that marked Mr. Punshon's time is the Metropolitan Church in the city of Toronto, and so large a part did he take in this enterprise that it is still pointed out as his monument in Canada." Assuredly, without him the Metropolitan Church would never have been built, nor would this great expense have been undertaken but for the support of strong and influential laymen. "Honour to whom honour is due." At one critical meeting of the trustees, when the tenders came in and the amount exceeded all expectations, there was a proposal to cut down the church in size. Even Dr. Punshon could not see the wisdom of proceeding on so extensive a scale. Then, a young man, Mr. James Paterson, rose, and in a few words, said, "We may cut down the plan, but we will not have a Metropolitan Church. Let us increase our subscriptions." And he quadrupled his own. His enthusiasm was at once caught up, and it was resolved to proceed with the work.

The erection of the Metropolitan gave an impulse to church building in Toronto amongst all the denominations. The largest and most beautiful of the one hundred churches in the chief city of Ontario, the City of Churches, have nearly all been erected since that time. In short, it revolutionized ecclesiastical architecture all over the Province. Along with this, more than any other minister he helped to promote

the sweet and fruitful spirit of Christian unity
so manifest among us. Incapable of narrowness
or bigotry, while his brilliancy and power drew
around him many outside the pale of Methodism,
his unfailing courtesy and the catholic spirit
which inspired his life was felt throughout the
churches, and they were drawn together in the
unity of spiritual life.

On the 23rd of September, 1870, his home was
again darkened by an overwhelming loss, in the
death of his beloved wife. The happiest of earthly
unions was severed. The desire of his eyes was
taken away at a stroke in the prime of her
strength and beauty, in the midst of her growing
influence and usefulness, and just as her happy
life was about to be crowned with the rich joy
of motherhood.

> " The sunshine of the heart was dead,
> The glory of the home was fled."

Her death startled and shocked a wide circle
of friends, and awakened emotions of profound
sorrow and regret among all who knew her. In
the midst of this desolation he was enabled to

6

say, " It is the Lord.   All Thy waves and Thy
billows are gone over me, but they are *Thy*
waves, and I lie and let them sweep, waiting
till Thou shalt tell me in the fulness of a clearer
vision why they sweep over me."

Returning from the funeral, one of the largest
ever seen in Toronto, he invited Dr. and Mrs.
Cochran, Professor Reynar, my wife and myself
to remain to tea with him.   When the time for
family worship came, as he opened the Bible to
read, he expressed his thankfulness to God that
he was again permitted to be the priest in his
shattered household.   He reviewed the past ten
years of his life, and paid a touching tribute to
his departed wife, her simple faith, earnest
piety, and unpretentious goodness, her sweet,
spotless life, the interest she had taken in all
his work, the deep and tender love which she
had shown to him and his children, and the
unutterable desolation that was upon him.   Yet
in his acquiescence with the Divine will he had
been saved from every rebellious thought.   He
then uttered his thanksgivings for family mercies yet remaining, his yearnings over his chil-

dren and his intense desire that not a shred of
the intended benefit of this great sorrow might
be lost upon any one of them. It was a striking
exhibition of the tenderest feeling that I ever
witnessed, and created an ineffaceable impression
on all present.

In the spring of 1871 Mr. Punshon made his
journey to the Pacific Coast. The party were
to have been joined by Mr. and Mrs. Joseph
Lister, of Hamilton, but " the father " could not
summon up courage to undertake the long and
arduous journey. On the eve of his departure
he addressed the following letter to Mr. Lister :

March 8, 1881.

MY DEAR SIR,—I have "dreamed a dream which is
not all a dream," or can it be that some bird of the air
has carried the tidings that there is a little relenting in
the mind of the inexorable "minority," and that the
august head of the household is a little more inclined
than he was to this Pacific trip.

The expedition will not leave Chicago until Tuesday,
21st March. One wishing to find a place for repentance
may obtain it by seating himself and *wife* (not otherwise)
in the Pullman car which passes through Hamilton on
Monday, 20th March.

Do this and you shall have all manner of absolutions and a pleasant journey westward, besides enjoying the refined luxury of giving great pleasure to

Your Affectionate Friend,

W. M. PUNSHON.

In his letters to his daughter and notes of travel he gives vivid descriptions of the great prairies, the Rocky Mountains, Salt Lake City, and the deceptions of Mormonism.

I shall never forget our entrance into Salt Lake Valley and the City of the Saints. We had been two days ascending the eastern slopes of the Rocky Mountains, and now made an abrupt and quick descent into this valley of the mountains. From snow-capped peaks we entered a deep and rocky ravine, thirty miles in length, and only a few yards in width, with a mountain wall on one side and precipitous overhanging cliffs on the other. Through the courtesy of the conductor we had been permitted to ride on the locomotive, or in the box-car, all the way down this Echo Canyon, and enjoyed to the full the scenery of this sublimest of mountain passes. From Echo we entered

Weber Canyon, another glorious pass, hewn by
Nature through the living rocks. On we rolled
past the Devil's Gate, where the Weber River

SALT LAKE CITY.

goes leaping and dashing and foaming against
high masses of rock, as though, buffeted from
mountain to mountain so long, it would rise up

in its angry strength and cleave the huge bar-
rier from base to summit to cut for itself a
channel to the sea. Still on we swept through
tunnels, over bridges, between overhanging
cliffs, waking the thundering echoes as we sped
along ; into rocky cuts and out of them, until
we were beginning to wonder if ever we should
have a safe escape from this wild and weird
descent, when lo! as by a sort of sudden surprise, the canyon widened into a lovely valley,
and our eyes were gazing with bewildered delight upon one of the purest and most perfect
landscapes which this whole earth can show.
We had entered Salt Lake Valley.

The Utah Railway, owned by the Mormons,
conducted us from Ogden, the terminus of the
Union Pacific Railway, to Salt Lake City. The
ride through that Valley, completely shut in by
natural barriers, was indeed charming. Everywhere were seen the changes which these working saints had wrought, for as by miracle they
have taken this uninhabited waste and transformed it from savage barrenness into a garden
—a wonder of the earth, the home of a thriving

people. All that this valley of alkali and dwarf
sage-brush needed was water to make it bud
and blossom ; and as we rode along we could
see channels cut from the snow-peaks down
into the farms, and catch the gleam of rills
glancing down the hill-sides, and meandering
through fields and vineyards. Flocks of sheep
dotted the terraced slopes, and dwelling-houses
stood on every side. I was seated beside a Mormon Elder who had one of his homes in Ogden,
and was going down to Salt Lake to spend
a little time with two of his wives living there.
His youngest wife was the teacher of Brigham
Young's school of children. We engaged in
conversation. I found him very communicative
and interesting. He had come into this valley
with the Mormon exodus from Council Bluffs,
in 1845, and he told me the story of their sufferings and privations as the weary caravan
dragged its way over the mountains to the
borders of this great inland sea. He told me
how sterile was the land and how dreary and
forbidding the prospect. But the land was consecrated to the Lord, the holy city was marked

out, and brawny arms and strong muscles had
turned the verdureless and desolate place into a
land flowing with milk and honey. It was

STREET IN SALT LAKE CITY.

night when we reached the city, and having got
comfortably established in the Townsend House,
"mine host" being a polygamous Mormon, we

were so weary that we sought rest at once. Next morning we were up bright and early. The day was brilliant and beautiful and the city was quiet in its Sabbath rest.

I shall never forget our first saunter through that embowered city. The air was soft and sweet, southern in its odour, northern in its freshness. The clear, pellucid waters of the mountain-brooks sparkled and rippled in the sunshine as they murmured along on each side of the broad avenues, shaded with acacias. The grand snow-crested mountains, brought near, so near, by the wondrous purity of the atmosphere, displayed every cleft and undulation in their bosoms, while their peaks and sides were draped with floating clouds as soft and white as the snow that wreathed them. Lower down in the valley a golden haze was steeping everything in its own delicious light. We started at once for the Mormon holy place—Temple Block, as it is called—in which are situated the old tabernacle, the great new one, with its rounded roof, looking like a huge oval dish-cover, and the foundations of the temple then in process of erection.

The New Tabernacle, which appears in the general view of the city, like a great meat platter for the Titans, with its oval cover, is two hundred and fifty feet long by one hundred and fifty wide, and will seat an audience of ten thousand. At the west end stand the great organ and choir, and in front of these are circular rows of seats for the Church dignitaries, and the stands from which they address the audience. Elder Woodruff, in his sermon that Sabbath morning, told us that they were the only true Church now on earth, for with the death of the apostles, the power of the priesthood, the gifts of prophecy and revelation, were taken away, and only restored in this glorious dispensation of Joe Smith. He told us all about the Book of Mormon, and that it was an additional revelation of equal authority with the Bible. In the afternoon the sacrament was administered, the elements being bread and water. They were offered to every member of the congregation, who received them, while the preacher, Orson Pratt,

the orator and champion polygamist, was deliver-
ing his discourse. In the evening Dr. Punshon
preached to a large and motley congregation, in
which he says, there were " Methodist Mormons,
Josephites, Godbeites, the Chief Justice, and a
large number of United States officers. Among
the congregation was Orson Pratt's first wife, a
pale, crushed woman, out of whose heart the joy
of life had been trampled by the system, and
who has lived apart for some years, rather than
sanction, by her presence, the invasion of her
home."

Some of the houses of this unique capital are
of goodly size and style ; but they are for the
most part, cottages, built of *adobe* (sun-dried
bricks), and stand back some thirty feet from
the road-side in trim little gardens, bowered with
trees, and smothered with roses and creepers ;
and the whole city, which covers a space of three
thousand acres, appears from a distant view like
a vast park with sylvan bowers, gardens, fruit
trees and running streams of water from the
mountain-sides.

The famous view is from Camp Douglas, which

is situated on one of the benches that rise behind the city, as clearly cut as the steps of a temple.

SALT LAKE CITY—FROM CAMP DOUGLAS.

The famed prospects of Europe cannot excel it, and it resembles the view of Lombardy Plains and the distant Alps from the pinnacles of the Cathedral at Milan. Around you are mountain ranges blazing in the brilliancy of a thousand variegated tints; before you a valley of sensuous beauty, sending back from its bosom the rays of sunshine in colours, shapes and shadows, that paint and pencil never realize; the city of these Latter-day Saints sleeping in the vast cradle of the brightly-tinted valley; southward the lake itself, with its amplitudes of blue, whose bosom, placid and motionless, glowed like a sheet of burnished gold; while farther beyond, the rose-pink hue of mountains on a sea-coloured sky, loomed up like sleeping giants from the mystic background. The air is wonderfully pure. The sky overhead has an infinite depth and distance; and the vapoury gold of the atmosphere, as it floats over the lake and valley in a languid dream, contrasts beautifully with the intense blue of the cloudless azure and the rosy surfaces of the encircling hills.

This new religion is a sort of Judaism galvanized into the mockery of life, and adapted to this century. Its physical circumstances are a copy of the Jewish ; and these American saints have founded their Jerusalem in a holy land, wonderfully like the ancient Judea. "Look," said Col. Morrow, the genial officer of the United States forces, as we stood on the commanding elevation at the Camp, "look at the resemblance. There is the Dead Sea, for it has no outlet and no life. Over yonder is lake Utah, which ought to be called the Lake of Tiberias, a body of fresh water emptying into it by a river called Jordan. And there beyond stands Nebo."

It is wonderful, the numbers that have come from Europe to this New Canaan. As we were being shown through the Temple and sacred places in Temple Block, the custodian said to me, "Isn't that Morley Punshon ?" I answered "Yes; how do you know him ?" "Oh," he answered, "I have often heard him preach in England." I asked whether he had come as a convert and pilgrim to this land. He assured me that he had. I inquired how he had made the journey over the mountains. And his laconic reply was, "Walloping bulls"—meaning that he had driven over an ox-team.

VERNAL FALLS, YOSEMITE VALLEY.

Of this marvellous deception of Mormonism,
Dr. Punshon says, "It may not be hastily dis-
missed as a vulgar imposture. It is a crafty and

powerful lie, and the fanaticism which it kindles in its votaries, has in it a generous chivalry, akin to that which dwelt in the Crusaders of old."

From Salt Lake City he crossed the Sierra Ranges to the El-Dorado State. San Francisco, the Queen City of the Pacific, is described; the Golden Gate, the exquisite coast and scenery of Vancouver Island, Victoria, New Westminster, the Fraser River as far as Yale, grandly situated, just like sweet Swiss villages; the Gulf of Georgia, the Big Trees and the Yosemite Valley, the two gems of which, the Yosemite Falls and the majestic El Capitan, moved him to tears. His knowledge of the famed prospects of Europe, his quick powers of observation and deep sympathy with nature, along with his unfailing good temper and characteristic ardour, made him a rare travelling companion; and this journey widened his experience of the outer aspects of the world and supplied him abundant material and illustrations for future use.

A messenger to the Churches in these distant regions he preached along the entire way, and was alike at home in growing cities, in Indian

POTLUI POSTS.

7

settlements and frontier towns. On his return
to Toronto he makes this record in his journal :

" May 26th.—Since my last entry, how marvellous have
been the preserving mercies of the Lord. I have to record many loving-kindnesses. I have taken a long journey. I have been preserved by land and sea, amid
many excitements, discomforts, and pleasures, through
8,800 miles of travel. . . . . I have been permitted 'to
testify for Christ, I humbly trust not without success, in
regions which I may never see again. My soul is full of
gratitude. . . ." P. 359.

On the first of June, 1871, his beloved daughter, Fanny, of whom he speaks as being by sorrows " sanctified into a very woman of truth and
purity," was married to the Rev. Professor Alfred
H. Reynar, M.A., the man of her affection, into
whose hands the father unhesitatingly trusted
her. At the Conference Dr. Punshon was not
only elected President, but nominated for President in 1872, and appointed Representative to
the British Conference. In July he sailed for
England, accompanied by his daughter and her
husband. His reception in the homeland was
of the most enthusiastic kind. The open session

of the Conference, at which he was introduced as the President and Representative of the Canadian Conference, was held in the Free Trade Hall, Manchester, which was filled to overflowing with an audience of six thousand, of which nearly one thousand were ministers. An English paper says:

" It would be difficult to analyze and define delicately the feeling of the vast mass of people who rose to greet him with shouts, and waving of hats, handkerchiefs, umbrellas, and all movable things. But I shall not be far wrong when I surmise that the predominant emotion was deep, personal affection, sympathy with his great services past, and joy at his return. English Methodists have kept his place vacant in their hearts." P. 363.

The address was one of the most eloquent and effective efforts of his life, and never before were the claims and interests of our Canadian work so fully and forcibly brought before the English public. The Conference set a term to his stay in Canada when he was to return home, and during his visit he was everywhere greeted with the warmest affection and expressions of esteem.

Among the many letters from him which I

cherish, I find one written at this time, bearing date :

LONDON, August 24, 1871.

MY DEAR FRIEND,---Thanks for your letter which I was right glad to receive. I cannot find time for correspondence amid my multiplied engagements and excitements, so my friends must not regard me as indifferent or forgetful, but simply as continually and overwhelmingly engaged. You will have seen the address at the Free Trade Hall. They say it told pretty well; and perhaps you will have seen also the Conference action, that it intimates an intention to "reclaim the loan." I moved neither eye, hand nor lip in this, and so far, therefore, it may be regarded as providential. It secures me in Canada at any rate for two years or thereabouts, but more of this anon. My reception has been more than cordial, it has been enthusiastic, and has much humbled me, as I think successes ought to do. I do not think Methodism is altogether as happy as it was wont to be in England, though there is much power about it yet.

I am glad to hear of your prosperity, and that the Metropolitan progresses well. I am trying to do a little for it here; but everybody has his own schemes, and their name is legion. I shall succeed a little.

Fanny and her husband are in Bristol at present. It has been a painful pleasure to revisit old scenes, and renew old friendships, but the Lord has kept me up until I had a brief collapse last Friday, and was unable to take two engagements. I lectured in Bristol, however, on Monday, and on Tuesday preached in Spurgeon's Tabernacle to 7,000 people, the grandest sight of human beings I ever gazed upon. Pray give my kindest regard to everybody—Ryersons, Green, Rose, Dewart, Sutherland, Griffin, Evans, etc., etc. Special to your bonnie wife, and believe me, my dear friend,

Yours most truly,

W. M. PUNSHON.

Early in September he returned to Canada, bringing with him his niece, Miss Panton, to keep up the light and warmth of his home, to fill the place of his "lost angel" and of his daughter, now gone to a home of her own. The biography here, it seems to me, does not adequately set forth the character of his work— attending missionary services, preaching, teaching and dedicating churches, among them the holy and beautiful house of his affection, the Metropolitan. As the time drew near for his departure, his friends in Canada who loved and honoured him became very urgent that he should remain, and he himself writes, "I shall be as sorry to leave Canada as I was to leave England." He was even offered a chair in Moral

Philosophy in the Toronto University, but he was constrained to decline the position. At the Convocation of Victoria University, in 1872, the Senate insisted upon conferring on him the degree of LL.D., the highest in its gift—a degree which has during nearly the half century of the University's existence been conferred *honoris causa* only thirteen times.

The last Conference in which he sat in the chair, June, 1872, was the most important of the five over which he had presided. Of it he says :

"Though there was much difference of opinion, there was substantial unity at last, and brotherly love throughout. Questions of difficulty were satisfactorily solved ; the commutation question amicably settled ; the principle of division of Conferences affirmed ; the way cleared for a union with the Conference of Eastern British America, and, if they so please, with the New Connexion ; and last, not least, it was decided to open a theological school in the City of Montreal."

From this to the end of the Conference year he was in journeyings often and in labours more abundant. He visited the Conference of Eastern British America and renewed the pleasant acquaintance made four years previously.

The gifted editor of the *Halifax Wesleyan,* the Rev. Dr. Lathern, has given a vivid account of Dr. Punshon's visit to the Eastern Provinces which we here subjoin :

The first effort of the Rev. Dr. Punshon, on his visit to the Eastern Provinces, in 1868, was the delivery of his lecture on "Daniel in Babylon," which was listened to by an audience, comprising the *élite* of the city of St. John, and it is sufficient to say, that the magnificent reputation which preceded the brilliant orator to this side of the Atlantic, was fully sustained on that occasion. The splendid audience was aroused to a point of irrepressible enthusiasm. The sermon which followed in the Centenary Church, on the Sunday morning, on " Let your light shine," abounding in splendid passages, and pervaded by a fine glow of spiritual feeling, took entire possession of the congregation, and is regarded still as one of the finest pulpit efforts that the city had ever known.

The immediate purpose of Dr. Punshon's visit to the Provinces, was to preside at the Conference of Eastern British America, appointed to meet that year in the city of Fredericton. It devolved upon the writer, as pastor of the Fredericton Church, and chairman of the District, to receive the distinguished preacher on his arrival at the capital. He was accompanied by Rev. Chancellor Nelles, and both were the guests, for the time, of Hon. Judge and Mrs. Wilmot, at their beautiful residence,

Evelyn Grove.   A lecture, an official address at the opening of Conference, and a noble speech at the Missionary Anniversary meeting, prepared the way for the Conference Sabbath.   Interest culminated on the occasion of the morning sermon.   All congregations were represented.   People came from distant towns and cities to listen to the peerless pulpit orator.   Looking out from the parsonage window, long before the hour for service, one could see that street and square were thronged with people, as if determined to take possession of the stately and beautiful Methodist sanctuary.   The spacious building, its aisles, galleries, and deepest recesses were densely crowded.   There could not be a grander sight than when that vast concourse of people chanted their *Te Deum Laudamus.*   The last of the English Lieutenant-Governors, and other distinguished persons were present.   The sermon was based upon the Saviour's reply to the Greeks, relating to an approaching crisis. It abounded in passages of philosophic reasoning, crystallized beauty of exposition, alternating with outbursts of oratory that thrilled the listening congregation.   It was a surprise to find that with all its affluence of expression, such was the accompaniment of spiritual power and truth, as applied, that admiration for the brilliance of the preacher was lost in absorbing and reverential interest of the theme, as then unfolded.

Nothing is more vividly remembered in connection with the Fredericton Conference, than the expressions of pleased surprise with which veterans of the Conference, able administrators, men of light and learning, were wont to refer to the practical ability exhibited by the gifted President, and his perfect acquaintance with all technical details and matters of business. Appreciation of the manner in which all official duties were discharged was unstinted. But it was felt that distinguished pulpit and platform services were worthy of the very highest recognition, and that through them all Methodist interests had been subserved.

After the close of Conference, one day was taken for absolute rest and recreation. What a memorable day that was at the Grove! It was at summer brightness, spent in the open air, beneath the grateful shade of the tall, dark pine trees, that formed the back-ground of the residence. Dr. Nelles was in his happiest mood. One or two other guests were privileged to enjoy the gladness of a day, which, in their experience, has not been duplicated. The Judge, then just appointed the first Governor of his native Province, was in brightest mood, and no one knew better than host and hostess how to crown with their courtesies and complete the happiness of their guests.

From Fredericton to St. John, Dr. Punshon was accompanied by the Governor and others. We had the privilege of listening to his lecture in the Centenary Church, on "John Wesley"; in which the closing passage was one of the finest and most triumphant efforts of his eloquence.

Accompanied by Dr. Nelles and his son, Dr. Punshon crossed the Gulf to Charlottetown. Anticipation was at its height. The Methodist Church there is the most capacious in the Lower Provinces. But on one of the hottest days of the season it was crowded to suffocation, and here the people, who knew well how to appreciate the best style of preaching, were electrified by the oratory of the inimitable preacher. He unfolded and amplified the meaning of the Apostle's affirmation : " This one thing I do," etc. An esteemed official brother of that Church says, the fervent appeals to the consciences of his hearers to follow St. Paul's example were probably never equalled in that sanctuary, before or since. For an hour the audience was held by the spell of the preacher, and at pauses in the sermon one could hear a sigh, as of relief from the intense and almost overpowering tension in which the people had been held by the preacher's eloquence. The impression of the pulpit effort was more than sustained by a magnificent platform oration, which followed on the next evening. Such an intellectual and even spiritual treat our brother (to whom I am indebted for reminiscences of the island visit, an honored member of more than one General Conference), never expects to hear again. It was a realization of Milton's exquisite ideal :

> " The angel ended, and in Adam's ear
> So charming left his voice, that he awhile
> Thought him still speaking, still stood fixed to hear."

For some years several laymen of the Charlottetown Methodist Church had felt the necessity of Methodism taking some step in the matter of education, and it was thought that perhaps Dr. Punshon's visit might in some way be utilized in furtherance of the object. Leading members of the Church were invited to meet him at the house of Mr. W. E. Dawson ; and, after spending some time in social intercourse, he introduced the matter in a few brief words, showing the inadequacy of the Government Schools—the insidious advance being made by Rome in her conventual schools, in which they were led to believe some twenty-five or thirty children of Methodist parentage were being educated, and the absolute need of some effort being made, unless they desired to see their children led Romewards. Interchange of thought took place, words of wisdom and counsel fell from the lips of Mr. Punshon (as also from Dr. Nelles, who formed one of the company), and before the company broke up, several thousand dollars were subscribed towards a fund for the erection of a Wesleyan day-school, resulting in the erection of the noble building known as the Methodist Academy, at a cost, including ground and furniture, of about $27,000 ; formally opened 9th January, 1871, in the presence of the leading citizens, with a staff of several teachers, and between one and two hundred scholars.

Space fails to attempt any reference to Dr. Punshon's visit to Halifax. Nor is it possible to speak at length of

his visit to Mount Allison educational institutions, and
the valuable services rendered by him towards the effort,
then being made, of securing College Endowment."

In July he started with John Macdonald, Esq.,
for Manitoba, on a missionary tour to the Great
North-West.   On Lake Superior he was in perils
of waters, which he thus vividly describes :

" Embarked on board the steamer *Manitoba*, called at
Goderich, Southampton, Bruce Mines, all on Lake Huron ;
passed through the St. Mary's river, and about six p.m.
on the eleventh went through the canal at Sault Ste.
Marie, which separates Lake Huron from Lake Superior.
A great wall of fog met us as we entered the latter, the
most enormous basin of fresh water in the world, unless
Lake Nyanza shall prove larger.   We toiled through
the fog all night.   About one p.m. on Thursday, the
twelfth, I was standing on the fore deck, the fog dense
and heavy, and the captain said to me, 'We are going
along like a pig in a poke.'   'More intelligently than a pig,
I hope,' was my reply, ' for you know where we are going.'
' Oh, yes,' was his answer.   The fog was coming down
heavily, so I retired into the saloon.   Not two minutes
after, I saw the captain rush frantically to the alarm bell
and reverse the engines.   At that moment the fog lifted,
and there was a desolate coast close upon us, towards
which we were driving at the rate of six miles an hour.
Two seconds only, as it seemed of agonizing suspense,

and the ship struck with a tremendous concussion, smashing crockery, glasses, doors, etc., flinging ladies down upon the floor, and causing, as you may suppose, immense consternation. For a moment the scene was terrible ; happily there was no rebound, and the vessel remained hard and fast upon the rocks. We found by-and-by we were on an island which was uninhabited, save at one end of it, some fifteen miles distant from the scene of our shipwreck. We all (one hundred and fifty) landed, made fires on the beach, or rather on the rock, found out lovely beaches, covered with the most exquisite quartz, spar, agates and amethysts, and so spent the day; the captain trying all manner of ways to get the boat off. At eleven next morning a sail was descried, which turned out to be the steamer *Cumberland,* bound for the same port as ourselves. She bore down to our rescue, and stayed with us for thirty hours in vain efforts to dislodge us. At length, on Saturday about six p.m., the *Manitoba* was pulled off the rocks, but alas, only to fill with water, so she was beached in about twelve feet of water, and all the passengers transferred to the *Cumberland,* in which we made the rest of our voyage."

At Fort Garry, now Winnipeg, he preached and conducted the first ordination service ever held by any Church in the North-West. He had a two days' conference with the missionaries, who were all present, and in a letter to his daughter he says :

"Some of the missionaries had come from 1,000 miles west to be with us. We gathered the whole nine or ten from each station, and had a blessed little conference One of them even had not seen a railway for twelve years. I felt so dwarfed in their presence. These are the true heroes of the Lord's host. I felt it almost presumption to assume any official position, and to counsel and question them ; I would gladly have sat at their feet. I trust our visit has done good. I have been much struck with the self-denial and earnestness of the missionaries, and with the vastness of the field they have to cultivate, especially in the great Saskatchewan country."

He saw "lots of Indians," was adopted into the Cree tribe, and received the name of " Wau-bu-nu-tiik," which means the "spirit of the morning." Returning, he journeyed through the Muskoka district, the lake scenery of which he characterizes as "exceedingly lovely." At Rama he attended an Indian camp-meeting, and was greatly interested in these children of the forest, keeping their Feast of Tabernacles. October was given to presiding over important committees—the Missionary Committee, comprising some eighty members, the Committee on Methodist Union, and the Committee on the division of Conference.

In November he was in Baltimore, dedicating the splendid Mount Vernon Church, one of the costliest churches in Methodism; where they offered him a salary of $5,000 per annum, and an elegantly furnished house, to become their pastor.

In December he was in Boston, preaching, lecturing, visiting Harvard University, and having a pleasant chat with Longfellow in his own study—"a fit lair for such a genius;" then to Stanstead, and on to Cobourg, to spend a few days with his daughter. Her health was now a subject of great concern to him, and the shadow of another sorrow was upon him. How he loved her is shown in a letter written at this time, full of birthday wishes, and greetings, and prayers, and closes with :

"God send His good angels to guard and bless thee, my child. From the weary morning in December, 1850, until now, when your child is dear to me, I have never ceased to cherish you in my heart of hearts, and I do not

cease now, although you have a happy home of your
own. May God bless it to you, and keep you to it for
many years. If my heart could go out upon the paper it
would burn. Again, God bless my darling child." P. 382.

About the middle of February he started on a
month's tour through the Southern States, and
he records more conscious waiting on God during
the journey than usual. He was accompanied
by H. A. Massey, Esq., of this city, then of Cleveland, Ohio ; and the following delightful account,
by Mr. Massey, of their visit to the sunny
South-land will be read with interest :

In January, 1873, the Rev. Dr. Punshon was engaged
to deliver a lecture for the benefit of the Ladies' Aid
Society of the First Methodist Episcopal Church, Cleveland, Ohio. The Doctor preached on the Sabbath morning to an overcrowded house, many hundreds not being
able to gain admittance ; and on Monday evening following, when the doors were thrown open for the lecture,
the rush for seats was so great that a number of police-
men had to be employed to keep the people back. It
was found many hundreds having tickets could not gain
admittance, and the only use made of the office for the
sale of tickets was to redeem the tickets of those who
could not get in, and many hundreds had to be bought
back. So great was the anxiety to hear his celebrated

lecture on "*Mayflower* Memories," that many offered
as high as $10 to get in, some having come seventy or
eighty miles to hear him, but they could not be accom-
modated. The lecture, there is no need to say, gave very
great satisfaction, and the Doctor was urged to repeat
it or give another lecture. He finally consented, with
the proviso that I should accompany him on his contem-
plated tour through the Southern States. This I consented to do, and after his second lecture, which was also
a great success, the Doctor proceeded to Cincinnati on
his way to the South, at which place I was to join him,
but this I was unable to do till he reached Louisville,
Ky. At Cincinnati the Doctor met with a very warm
reception from the leading citizens, and had a very large
audience at his lecture there.

At Louisville we met Bishop Simpson, and had a very
pleasant interview. The Doctor's high regard for Bishop
Simpson led him to look upon him as one of his dearest
friends, and he spoke of the Bishop as having no equal in
the pulpit in his magnetic influence over his hearers.
We drove out to the suburbs of Louisville, and were
delighted to find the contrast in the foliage of the trees
and shrubs, and the beauty of the grounds, so great in
comparison with those of the north. Places we had left
a few days before were cold and dreary, and in this
southern latitude it was warm and sunny. In the cemetery we found flowers in full bloom—magnolias flourishing
in great abundance. From Louisville we proceeded by

8

train to Nashville, where we spent two or three hours of the time in rambling through the quaint old city.

After leaving Nashville, our train got stuck on a very heavy grade, necessitating the dividing of the train, one portion being sent forward to the next station while the other remained till the engine came back for it. In consequence of this mishap we were without our breakfast till we arrived at Memphis. The Doctor and I made the best use of our time while we were stuck on the grade in making a foraging expedition to the log cabin of a coloured family, where we were treated with the greatest kindness ; and they gave us the best of what they had, which assuredly was very meagre, yet it was greatly enjoyed by us. We had thus an opportunity of viewing the humble homes of those who but a few years before were slaves, and the Doctor took very great interest in their stories of former bondage.

We arrived after midnight at Memphis, and in the morning proceeded to our steamer, the *Thompson Dean*, which had just arrived and was lying at the dock, and engaged our passage to New Orleans. Memphis being a very important shipping point on the Mississippi, large quantities of cotton and other products were loaded upon our steamer. The *Thompson Dean* is one of the largest vessels on the line, very fine in all her appointments, in reality a floating palace. There were a large number of passengers on board on their way to New Orleans to be present at the Mardi Gras. Many of the young people were full of fun and frolic, and determined upon having a good time, which they certainly did ; music and dancing going on most of the time. On one occasion they had a masquerade dance, all those taking part being completely disguised, causing much amusement to the passengers. We had quite a number on board who did not join with them, and with whom we had much pleasure in conversation and singing, there being a number of very good singers on the steamer.

The river at this time was beginning to rise rapidly, in consequence of the thaws and rains that were taking place along its tributaries. As we proceeded down the Father of Waters, we noticed that it had overflown its banks and had largely inundated forests and low-lying lands in all directions. There is much similarity in the scenery along the whole route, woods occupying a large portion of the ground, with log huts interspersed here and there. We often stopped at the side of the river to obtain wood where not a solitary person is living. At this season of the year fogs are quite frequent, and one night we had to stop for several hours and tie up to a tree along the bank of the river.

Our first stopping place of any importance after leaving Memphis was Vicksburg, where we arrived at 7 a.m. The Doctor and I walked around the city, and went upon the heights to see the breastworks, which were prepared during the late Civil War. This place was one of very great importance during the war, and will be

remembered as the place where Grant won his first great
victory.   We left Vicksburg at 9 a.m. calling at Natchez,
and Baton Rouge, which used to be the capital of the
State, a fine old English-looking place. The ruins of the
old Capitol stands upon a high point of the city, and have
an imposing appearance.

While on our passage down the river, I was waited
upon by a deputation of the passengers, who, notwithstanding their gaiety, love of dancing and card playing,
were eager to secure the services of Dr. Punshon to
preach upon the following Sabbath. He consented to
do so. This sermon was preached soon after leaving
Baton Rouge, that day being Sunday, and all were delighted with it.   It was delivered to a very large audience,
as there were many hundreds of people on board, a
large portion being Roman Catholics. After the service
the passengers met together, presided over by a leading
Roman Catholic editor, and passed resolutions of thanks
to the Doctor for his appropriate and eloquent sermon.

We arrived at New Orleans late on Sunday night,
and on Monday morning we were met at the steamer by
the Rev. Dr. Tudor, pastor of the First Church South, in
New Orleans, and R. W. Royne, Esq., a wealthy gentleman of that city. The latter invited us to be his guests
during our stay, and we gladly accepted the kind invitation, as the city was so full of strangers that no rooms
could be obtained for any price at the hotels. Dr. Tudor
had arranged for Dr. Punshon to either lecture or preach

for his people without the Doctor's consent, and it was with very great reluctance that he yielded to the very urgent solicitations of many of the leading people of that city, as he was away from home for rest, and had resolved not to lecture during his tour. He finally consented to preach for them, which he did on Monday evening, the 24th, to a very large audience.

New Orleans at this time was in a great state of excitement, immense preparations having been made for their annual festival, or *Mardi Gras*, and to one who had never before witnessed that gorgeous procession, it was certainly something to be admired and remembered. The Doctor was very much amused by many of the scenes as they passed in procession through the streets. During the evening the display was simply grand. We visited many of the ice manufacturing establishments of that city, and were much interested in witnessing the process of making that very useful and necessary commodity of this warm climate. The thermometer stood on this day, the 25th of February, 70° in the shade. We visited the cemetery, where they bury their dead in vaults above ground, as the land here is lower than the river level. The public buildings are all very fine, and we think well worth visiting.

We left New Orleans on the morning of the 26th for Mobile, Ala. Very little of interest was to be seen on this route, with the exception of a few alligators. The country through which we passed on our way to Mobile is very low and flat, the sandy soil poor and unproductive, and very little is grown except cotton, of which there are large plantations cultivated by the coloured people. We also noticed several large sugar plantations.

At Mobile we were unable to secure sleeping berths for the night, consequently we had to make the best of it, under which circumstances the Doctor proved a patient traveller, and submitted with becoming grace to the many inconveniences we had to endure. At Columbus we had another delay of several hours.

The presiding elder of the Methodist Church South waited upon the Doctor and pressed him to preach in the evening. We visited some cotton mills and other manufacturing industries along the Chattahoochee River, and the Quarterly Conference of the Methodist Church, which was then in session. In company with the presiding elder we visited, at his home, the venerable Dr. Lovick Pierce, then in his 89th year, and who had preached as an effective minister uninterruptedly for 67 years, his last sermon being on the previous Sabbath. He held the position of Missionary editor. We sat for a half-hour or more, while Dr. Pierce delighted us with reminiscences of Wesley in Savannah, and of Methodism in general. When about leaving, Dr. Pierce expressed his gratification at having enjoyed the great privilege of an interview with his friend, Dr. Punshon, when the Doctor replied, " I am honoured, sir, to sit and learn wisdom from age."

Arriving at Savannah on Saturday morning, we called upon the Methodist minister and took him for a drive out to Bonaventura, where we saw some of the most beautiful oaks in the world. For a long distance the drive was between rows of these magnificent trees, whose branches formed a complete arch over the street, and shaded it from the hot sun, which made it very enjoyable. After viewing the cemetery and grounds, we visited the large oak under which Wesley preached, and drank out of the Wesley spring. The memories of Wesley's labours around this hallowed spot were inspiring to us all, especially to the Doctor, as he eagerly grasped every opportunity that offered of securing any information relative to Wesley's work in this locality. He also searched the city records for the purpose of gleaning some particulars relative to his labours in that city, in which he was somewhat successful. When we entered the church, which is now built upon the spot where Wesley preached, we felt an inspiration which will not soon be forgotten.

The next day, Sunday, March 2nd, the Doctor preached in Trinity Church, his subject being, "I count all things but loss for the excellency of the knowledge of Christ Jesus my Lord;" and a truly noble sermon it was. The Doctor afterwards said he felt a special inspiration in preaching on the spot which had been the first field of Wesley's labours many years ago. In the afternoon I accompanied the Doctor to the coloured church, as he was very anxious to attend the meetings of the coloured people. In some of these meetings the services were very boisterous and exciting, as they are a very emotional people; yet the Doctor' enjoyed them all exceedingly, and could rejoice with them in their forms of worship. In the evening we went to the Presbyterian Church.

Leaving Savannah on Monday morning, we arrived at Jacksonville the same evening. On the road through Florida we were favoured with an almost continuous display of wild flowers and blossoms. At Jacksonville the next morning we found the weather quite cold, so much so that ice about the one-eighth of an inch thick had formed upon the water. We took a steamer up the St. John River to Tricola, and from there, horse rail to St. Augustine, where we remained over night. This ancient city was very much admired by the Doctor. We visited the old fort and some orange groves, picking ripe fruit from the trees. This old Spanish city has many places of historic interest, and the climate is delightful. The Doctor was particularly interested in going through some of the cells in the old fort, and here we purchased a number of curiosities. We left on the early morning train, on our return journey, arriving at Jacksonville that evening, from whence we took train to Savannah, on our homeward route, arriving at Charleston on Thursday evening, where we stayed for the night, and went to a prayer-meeting held by the coloured people. Next morning found us *en route* to Washington. In passing Petersburg, we saw much of the fighting ground and

had a view of other battle-fields during the Civil War.
Had a very good view of Richmond, and arrived at
Washington on Saturday evening.

The Doctor was desirous of keeping very quiet, and
of not having it known that he was in the city. I had,
however, telegraphed Rev. Dr. Tiffany our intention of
spending the Sabbath in Washington. Sunday morning
Dr. Tiffany called on us at our hotel, and insisted on Dr.
Punshon preaching, and with difficulty did we prevail on
him to preach. We knew well the anxiety of many of
the great statesmen there to hear him in the evening. We
attended the Metropolitan Church in the morning, sitting
in one of the back seats, as the Doctor desired not to be
observed among the congregation. It was announced by
Dr. Tiffany that Dr. Punshon would preach in the evening, and pew-holders would be admitted by ticket at the
rear entrance. President Grant intimated to Dr. Tiffany
his anxiety to hear Dr. Punshon, although, as he stated,
he generally stayed at home on Sunday evening, so as
to allow his servants an opportunity to go to church. He,
however, was present that evening, and had great difficulty to get through the immense crowds that pressed
around both of the street entrances to the church.
There were a larger number of people that could not
gain entrance than those who were privileged to listen
to him on that occasion. Although much fatigued from
travelling, the peerless preacher was in his happiest
mood, and delighted his audience with his masterly dis-

course. President Grant was so delighted, that on leaving the church he said to Dr. Tiffany, " You will please
convey my sincerest thanks to Dr. Punshon for his magnificent sermon, which I have enjoyed so much."   There
were a great number of the Senators and Congressmen
present at this service.

On Monday we visited the Post Office, the Treasury
Department and also the Capitol, where the Doctor was
met by many leading statesmen, to whom he was introduced, and not a few of them expressed their gratification
at meeting so distinguished a man. After leaving Washington we came on to Baltimore, where I spent the last
evening of my journey in the Doctor's company with
some of his friends."

From Washington Dr. Punshon wrote as follows to Mrs. Lister, of Hamilton, describing
Southern habits and scenery :

WASHINGTON, D. C., March 10, 1873.

MY DEAR MRS. LISTER,—I am on my homeward
journey at last, and feel inclined to let you know that
although I have lacked your much-desired and "motherly"
care, I am still in the land of the living. I have had no
one but Mr. Massey, of Cleveland, as my companion.
My Canada friends, you see, are dropping off from me. I
went to Buffalo, as you know, thence to Cleveland, Akron,
Cincinnati. At the latter city, where the water is of the
colour and consistency of pea-soup before you wash in it,

and afterwards of lamp-black oil, I was seized with a
sharp attack of lumbago, an inauspicious beginning. I
persevered, however, and went to Louisville, Kentucky,
where Mr. Massey joined me. We railed to Nashville,
and thence through Tennessee to Memphis. Here we
took the *Thompson Dean*, and steamed down the Mississippi 824 miles, through the States of Mississippi,
Arkansas and Louisiana, passing and calling at Vicksburg, Natchez and Baton Rouge, to New Orleans. The
hardest thing I have had to do for some time was to
preach in the saloon of a Mississippi steamer to a congregation, most of whom had been dancing as if bitten by
a Naples spider, until midnight on Saturday night.

At New Orleans we were welcomed and entertained
with true Southern hospitality, and came in for the festival of the Carnival, which it would take too long to
describe. From New Orleans (where overcoats were an
unmitigated nuisance, and the heat was oppressive), to
Mobile in Alabama; thence to Montgomery and Columbus, in Georgia, where we missed connections, and had
to wait 24 hours. I had not been a quarter of an hour
in the hotel before a long brother called, who introduced
himself as the Presiding Elder, and said there was a union
love-feast going on, and I must come and talk to the
people. In for it again. I had been recognized at the
depot by some one who had heard me in Brooklyn.

From Columbus to Savannah, a fine city, where there
is the most appropriate cemetery I ever saw, for nature

has furnished the mourning. There are long avenues of fine old oaks, from each branch of which hang pendant wreaths of Spanish moss of a sombre olive hue—natural immortelles over the graves of the loved and lost. I preached in Savannah just opposite the spot where John Wesley preached, and tried to speak as he and his Master would have had me speak.

From Savannah down into Florida, weather very cool, almost cold; down the St. John River to St. Augustine, frost on the ground; the trees laden with oranges, superb magnolias, palmettoes, figs, bananas, live oaks, a blooming wilderness; back to Savannah, and up to Charleston, South Carolina; through North Carolina and Virginia, passing Petersburg, the last Citadel of the Confederacy; Richmond, the capital; Fredericksburg, where some of the bloodiest battles were fought, and Guinea, where Stonewall Jackson died; then sailing up the Potomac past Mount Vernon, where rest the ashes of the Father of his country, and arriving here on Saturday night, in time yesterday to address a few words of counsel to the President of the United States, who was in my congregation last night.

As the time of separation drew near he writes :

" I am wonderfully attached to this place and people. It will be a pang for me to leave Canada. It will always be endeared to me by memories of joy and sorrow, of usefulness and solicitude. I have made many friendships here which will abide."

Early in April, his beloved friend, Rev. Mr. Hurst, came out to be with him, to lighten the sorrows of parting, and accompany him home. On the eighth of May he writes, " The pangs of parting have already begun, and they are hard to bear."   On the eleventh, he preached his fare-well sermon in the Metropolitan Church, and among his last words to the congregation were these :

" The long bond which has united us is now of necessity loosened. From other lips you will listen to the words of eternal life.   Our interest in each other, fresh and vivid and hearty now, will become by a law that is common, and of which therefore we may not complain, fainter and fainter, until down the corridors of memory we must gaze, to recall with an effort the names and circumstances that are so familiar to-day ; but deeply in a heart that does not soon or readily forget will be graven in dis-tinctest lettering, the name of this house of prayer and of the congregation that has gathered within its walls."

Before his departure he was entertained by a large number of Canadian friends, and a testi-monial was given him as a slight proof of their affection and esteem, and of the value which they set upon the services he had rendered to the Methodist Church and to Canada. An illuminated address was presented, and a casket composed of several kinds of Canadian woods, mounted with clasps and plate of solid silver, and containing $4,000. His reply was given with deep feeling, and he accepted the money only on condition that it should be invested in Canada, that he should draw the interest until his death, when the principal should be applied to the Superannuated Ministers' Fund. He went by the Royal Mail steamer to Montreal, and the wharf was crowded with troops of friends assembled to bid him good-bye, and he sailed away encompassed with their love and followed by their most fervent prayers.

> " And women's tears fell fast as rain,
> And strong men shook with inward pain,
> For him they ne'er should see again."

At Cobourg came the never-to-be-forgotten parting between the father and the daughter ; they were not to meet on earth again, for in the following July, the tender daughter, the beloved wife, the true-hearted friend, slept in Jesus. At

Kingston he was met by a deputation and presented with an address. At Brockville the District Meeting adjourned to the wharf to bid him farewell.

On the 24th May, 1873, he sailed from Quebec on the S. S. *Sarmatian*, encircled with the Christian sympathy and affection of two nations on this side of the Atlantic. His work in Canada was finished, and what a work! Most tersely put by the Hon. Senator Macdonald, who, in reply to a question put by the late Sir William McArthur, of London, "Well, what did Mr. Punshon do for you when he was in Canada?" answered, "Do for us? Why, he pushed us on half a century."

And here let the Hon. John Macdonald himself speak, for he has written a most valuable letter giving his estimate of Dr. Punshon's character and a comprehensive view of his administration and work here, which will be read with absorbing interest as coming from one closely associated with him in Church enterprises, and favoured with so large a share of his inestimable affection.

Mr. Macdonald wrote from the Senate as follows:

OTTAWA, April 6, 1888.

MY DEAR MR. JOHNSTON,—You ask me to give you my own impressions of the work and character of the Rev. Dr. Punshon, as I knew him in Canada.   How difficult it is to do this appropriately.   His *first* public appearance, if I remember right, was at the Richmond Street Church, on the occasion of the departure of the Rev. George Young, now Dr. Young, to Fort Garry, and E. R. Young to Beren's River, then to a large extent an unknown country, where the missionary, it was supposed, would have to endure great privations.   Who, in the great company assembled on that occasion in the Old Cathedral of Methodism, will ever forget the magnetism of the speaker or the power which accompanied that address? Many there were who had never felt until then the heritage which, as Methodists, we possessed in our own hymns as he quoted the lines—

"And if our fellowship *below*
   In Jesus be so sweet,
What *heights* of rapture shall we know,
   When *round* His throne we meet?"

That address from such a man at such a time had an effect, the result of which it is difficult to estimate.

There were brethren—cautious brethren, good brethren, but fearful brethren—who thought the action of sending men to the North-West premature; who thought that "the time was not yet;" who thought that the work nearer home demanded greater attention, and that the work in Fort Garry might well be delayed.

When Dr. Punshon sat down, amid the manifestations of delight of that great company, there was not one there, however doubtful he may have been before, who did not feel that the movement was in the right direction, that "the cloud was lifted up," and that the Church was directed to go forward. How can we, as we look at the marvellous development of the work in the North-West, dissociate the new life, and the new energy, and the new inspiration created by that powerful appeal, or fail to realize how inseparably it is connected with the success of our work in that country to the present time. Although the occasion referred to was one of those rare instances in the life of any man which awakens in him a spirit of inspiration, and calls forth the best efforts of which he is capable; yet this same spirit largely marked all his platform efforts. He never said anything upon any of these occasions which was not well said, and was so exhaustively treated as to leave but little for those who followed him.

Methodism has been greatly favoured in Canada in the class of men who have preached its doctrines. Its earlier men (many of them at least) were rough as the forests through which they rode on their interminable circuits; plain of speech, with no great amount of the

9

learning of the schools; but true of heart and honest as the sunlight, they were deservedly welcomed by the scattered settlers in their humble but hospitable homes. How much they have had to do with causing " the wilderness and the solitary place to be glad, and the desert to rejoice and blossom as the rose," no thoughtful man will find it difficult to determine. They were honest, plain men, dealing in plain Anglo-Saxon, and never afraid to expose not the wrong only, but the wrong-doer.

But with the coming of Dr. Punshon amongst us there burst upon us a class of sermons to which we had not been accustomed to listen, and the desire to hear him was widespread beyond the bounds of his own denomination. His fame from beyond the sea had preceded him; enquiries were made by many, " Is there any chance of my getting a seat?" Long before the time of service the building in which he was to officiate, however large, was filled, and, from the beginning to the end of the service, the great congregation hung upon his lips. Why was this? Was there anything sensational about his style? He abhorred sensationalism — any effort to exalt the man. He was modesty itself. What was the secret of his wonderful popularity in the pulpit or on the platform? His theme was Christ, and Christ always! The Gospel which he preached was the same Gospel that the rough, plain, honest pioneers, to whom I have alluded, preached in their own rough, plain, honest way in the early days, but there was this difference—they produced a plain picture, his touches made the same picture radiant with life, so that it literally flashed with beauty, and when the service was completed, there was the conviction that something new had been learnt from the treasury of God's Word.

One has seen the whole aspect of a locality transformed by the skill of the landscape gardener. One has seen the streets and squares of a city invested with new beauty by the skill of the architect. With just such new interest were his pulpit ministrations invested, so that no one who came sincerely desiring to be edified—may I not add, that no one coming even with great expectations—ever went away disappointed.

Two instances occur to me which illustrate the desire of the people to hear him. The first was at the opening of a new church near Streetsville. The day proved to be one marked by such a snow-storm as under ordinary circumstances would have deterred people from facing it. Long before the hour of service, the country side lines were alive with teams conveying great numbers of people. These speedily filled the church and the basement, as well as the old church, while great numbers found it impossible to get even into the old building, and were obliged to return. Dr. Punshon preached in the new church. The pastor preached in the old one, and, as stated, numbers were unable to get into either building. The other occasion was one in which this desire to hear him was not only manifested, but, also, strikingly illustrated by the fidelity with which he filled his engagements. He had arranged to preach in the Bloor Street Church (now the Central Methodist Church). Early on the morning of the Sabbath to which this notice refers, one of the most terrible storms which ever visited the city broke over it, and continued to rage with great fury for many hours. Distinct shocks were felt in many parts of the city. The Parliament Street Church was badly wrecked. The belfry of the Baptist Church, Yonge Street, was blown down; several buildings in course of erection were destroyed. The Roman Catholic Cathedral, almost in front of his own house, was badly damaged, portions of the spire being torn away and carried through the roof. The rain literally came down in great sheets, the streets were deserted, the churches were empty; no cabman could be induced to venture into the storm,—he would have been justified had he remained at home; waiting, in expectation that some one would come for him, until he felt that he could wait no longer, he tried himself to secure a cab. No cab could be obtained. He started out,—reached the church literally drenched in the storm, and so soon as he could obtain a change of clothing and a pair of slippers (for he could not get boots), which he did from a gentleman whose house was next to the church, preached to *a full congregation*, which had come through that terrible storm to hear him that morning. Well were they repaid as he spoke to them from the words of the Saviour, and the reply of Peter, as found in John vi. 66–68: "From that time many of His disciples went away and walked no more with Him. Then Jesus said unto the twelve, Will ye also go away? Then Peter answered Him, Lord, to whom shall we go? Thou hast the words of eternal life."

The great church building movement in Ontario dates from the period of the erection of the Metropolitan Church. If this should be doubted by anyone, let them take the trouble to ascertain the date of the erection of the splendid churches which adorn the City of Toronto; let them ascertain when the churches in every city, town, and hamlet in Ontario, which are pretentious and modern in their character, were erected, and they will find, with very few exceptions, that they date *after* the Metropolitan Church. The movement assumed something of the form of an epidemic, and not confined to the Methodist Church, for it seized all the denominations, and churches began to arise, beautiful in their architecture, commodious in their internal arrangements, and so admirably adapted for church work, with their schools and class-rooms, that it may with fairness be claimed that to-day Canada, in the number, beauty, and arrangement of its churches, stands *ahead of any country in the world.*

It is, I think, freely conceded that in the spirit of enterprise awakened in all the churches, by the erection of the Metropolitan Church, this movement had its origin—a movement which is still being carried on with increased energy.

The question arises, then, Who was the inspiring spirit

in the erection of the Metropolitan Church? To this question, I think, there can only be but one reply, viz. Dr. Punshon! To claim that the effort was due solely to him would be unfair, but it would be safe to assert that without him its building at that time would have been an impossibility. I am glad to bear testimony to the fact, familiar as I was with the enterprise from its inception to its completion, that to the late Rev. Dr. Ryerson, the late Mr. W. T. Mason, and Mr. James Paterson, of the City of Toronto, much was due in securing to the body a church such as the Metropolitan, instead of one greatly inferior, and which could scarcely be regarded as a representative building. To Dr. Punshon the credit of the Metropolitan, in its present form, chiefly belongs. In aiding the effort by his great name and great influence, in liberally contributing his own means, and by means secured for it by his own personal effort from his own personal friends, by the handsome sum presented as the result of his lecture, amounting to about one thousand dollars, by the consciousness on the part of the public that his whole being was interested in the movement, these were powerful factors in the successful completion of this great undertaking. This being so, it is not difficult to understand that to him are we not only indebted for a new departure in pulpit services, but that to him mainly belongs the credit of stimulating all denominations to that wonderful extension of church buildings, which are at once the pride and the glory of our land.

His gifts as a presiding officer were many and rare. They were marked by great firmness, great kindness, and excellent judgment. I had opportunities of knowing, as few of his brethren did, how earnestly he sympathized with them in their labours, and how anxiously he desired their comfort.

The annual meetings of the Missionary Committee were always to him, as they were, indeed, to all who took part in them, occasions of great interest; the precise condition of every mission, domestic and foreign, was carefully examined; the wants of the workers and the amounts available to meet the demands of each field were duly considered. At everyone of these gatherings, during his stay with us, he presided with an ability that was matter of common remark,—with a fairness that never was questioned. Upon these occasions I was always asked by him to take a place by his side. Before him was a schedule of what was needed, showing what was asked, what was proposed to be raised by each mission; not only did he understand the work for which the money was asked, but in most instances did he know the workers, and no remarks were more common during those sittings than some such as the following which he would whisper to me: "I wish we could do something more for him, — he is a good brother;" "It is impossible that the brother can live upon that amount;" "This is a weak cause, and must be liberally sustained for a year or two." As a counsellor he was always safe, and I am unable to remember a single suggestion made by him at any of these gatherings in which he did not carry the committee with him.

It was at the Missionary Committee, held in St. Catharines, that it was resolved definitely to enter upon the Japan Mission. It had been brought before the Committee held the preceding year, and failed; it was argued at the St. Catharines meeting, but met with considerable diversity of opinion. At a favourable point of the debate a slip was handed to him on which was written, " If it was tried now it would carry." He wrote on the slip and returned it, " The chief difficulty is the man; if we had him I would be more hopeful," or words to that effect. (This paper, so full of significance, is in my possession.) It being the last subject of debate, he said: "Brethren, let us pray to-night about this matter; we will then be better able to judge in the morning." The morning came, the matter was brought up, and the Church through its Missionary Committee had committed itself to the establishment of a mission in Japan. How wonderful have been the results of that action; how the fears of all the brethren who opposed it (conscientious as they were) have proved groundless; how it has surpassed all the sanguine expectations of those who promoted it; how it has stimulated the great missionary enterprise of our Church; how it has led to the formation of our invaluable Woman's Missionary Association; how it has intensified the missionary spirit in all the sister Churches, is matter of history.

I want just here to express my own great regret that we have no arrangements by which verbatim reports of all these important gatherings, in which great questions, such as the establishment of important missions, could be taken and preserved in book form, as the Hansard reports, for example, of the House of Commons are, what a heritage they would prove to us; what an invaluable link in the chain of Methodist history; what a treasury in giving us the thoughts of the great leaders of our Church —thoughts which now live only in the memories of those who heard them uttered, but which ought to be in a form which could be handed down to our children, and to our children's children; need I say that the result would be worth the expenditure many times told.

He loved Canadian Methodism, but he was full of sympathy for the work of the parent body, with which he had been so long connected; he felt a keen interest in the vast work to which it was committed, and sympathized with the Committee in reference to the debt which hindered the expansion of its work. Hence, when the proposal was made to him that the £1,000 sterling, which the parent body had undertaken to pay annually to the Canadian Conference, on its assuming the charge of the Indian Missions in the Hudson Bay territory, should be commuted for the sum of £3,000, that being the amount of the debt of the Missionary Society of the Canadian Methodist Church at that time, and a further sum of £1,500, the latter amount only to be asked for if urgently needed. Having unbounded faith in the ability of the Methodist Church of Canada to do its own missionary work, he gladly caught the idea of the commutation of the yearly grant by a present payment of £3,000, but objected to the £1,500, upon the ground that the wants of the parent Society were greatly in excess of the means at its disposal, that Canada was better able to do without that amount than the parent Society was able to pay it, although it would not hesitate to recognize the obligation if pressed; and so, as the result of his own suggestion—which was undoubtedly a good one—the settlement was made on the basis of £3,000 sterling, say in round numbers about $15,000.

Who can forget the zeal with which he threw himself into the endowment movement of Victoria College, and the results of the first meeting in Cobourg, due entirely to his own enthusiasm, while every subsequent meeting caught the inspiration which emanated from him. After the wonderful deliverance vouchsafed to those members of the deputation to Fort Garry on board of the steamer *Manitoba*, when shipwrecked on the Island of Michipicoten, in Lake Superior, it was felt that a thanksgiving service should be held on board the steamer *Cumberland*, the vessel which rescued us; but it was also felt that something more than words should express the thankfulness of the members of the deputation, and accordingly a subscription, in the form of a thank-offering, was taken up towards the erection of the Prince Arthur's Landing church (now Port Arthur), in which he appeared as one of the largest subscribers. The party went to the beautiful site where the church now stands ; a post, pointed at the end, was prepared, and with a heavy mallet each subscriber gave it a blow, driving it home, which answered for the ceremony of laying the foundation stone. The amount raised upon the occasion was something about $500. To many, no doubt, these circumstances may be unknown, yet this was the origin of the Port Arthur church.

At the Guelph Missionary Committee Meeting a movement was started to secure an educational institution or the North-West, in connection with our own Church. It was the intention to call it the Morley Institution. A sum of more than $2,000 was raised upon the spot. Had this amount been invested in land, supplemented, as it should have been, by a grant from the Hudson Bay Company, the promise of which I had from the Hon. Donald A. Smith. then Governor of the territory, now Sir Donald A. Smith, what an institution might we not have had to-day ; but, alas ! the money intended as the nucleus of an endowment being *spent for current expenses* was speedily exhausted, and the hope of an educational establishment, which would have equalled anything in that country, dissipated.

He was absent from Toronto when the movement was inaugurated to raise a purse on the occasion of his leaving Canada, as a slight token of the esteem in which he was held by his many friends. When he heard of this he was greatly distressed. Calling upon me (I think, on his way from the station,) he said that "he had learnt of this from the papers on his way home in the cars for the first time, that he felt greatly exercised about it, and begged that it might be stopped." He was told that that could not be ; and if it could, it would be unfair to his friends, who were deeply interested in the matter. He stated that while it was very good of his friends, yet if it was not too late, to stop it ; but if it must go on that he wished it to be understood that he could not take the money from Canada, that he would consent to accept the interest, with the understanding that at his death the principal would revert to the Superannuated Ministers' Fund.

The casket in which the address was enclosed, made from inlaid specimens of Canadian woods, he greatly prized, reminding him, as it always did, of his work in Canada. To the writer he pointed to it on the occasion of a visit to him at Brixton, saying at the same time how highly he prized it.

I might go on multiplying incidents, but these will doubtless be found in his biography by Rev. F. W. Mac donald, and by Professor Reynar, as well as in the sketch which you yourself are furnishing of his life and labours in Canada. One thing I must not omit to mention, and that is, that while I always found him ready to speak approvingly of the work, and the ability of his brethren, always ready to tell of the esteem and confidence in which he held them, I never yet upon any occasion heard him make one unkind statement, expressing lack of confidence in any brother, or utter one word which might be construed to a brother's disadvantage. He loved his brethren ; and I have reason to believe, was beloved by them in return.

Lives of men are not measured by years. It is by the life lived, the works wrought, the influences begotten, that the real value of one's life is to be estimated ; judged by this standard, what a life was his. I speak now only of the Canadian part of it. What mighty agencies was he the means of awakening ; what forces was he the means of quickening ; what a marvellous impetus did he give to every interest of the Methodist Church—the force of which is felt to-day throughout our entire work, and which will continue to be felt so long as time will endure.

What a lesson does the removal of such a man bring to us, called away when, to all human appearance, he was most needed ; when his matured wisdom and his safe judgment made him the wise counsellor and the safe judge. Then the Lord said to him, as He said to Moses,

"The day approacheth when thou must die." Mystery! Mystery! God's ways are not our ways. He doeth all things well. "He buries his workmen, but carries on His work." He was found ready for the summons, and entered into the joy of his Lord.

> " Oh, may we triumph so,
>   When all our warfare's past,
> And dying, find our latest foe
>   Under our feet at last."

I am, my dear Mr. Johnston,

Very truly yours,

JOHN MACDONALD.

IV.

ON the third of June, 1872, Dr. Punshon landed in Liverpool, and resumed again his citizenship and his ministry in England, his native land which he loved with a passionate affection that "many waters could not quench."

His first appearance was in London, in the old City Road Chapel, where he preached on a Tuesday afternoon, in aid of the liquidation of the debt on Westminster Chapel. The collection on this occasion was the largest ever made in a Methodist Chapel in England, amounting to £2,079—over $10,000. The discourse was founded on Psalm cxxxii. 8, 9. "Arise, O Lord, into Thy rest; Thou, and the ark of Thy strength. Let Thy priests be clothed with righteousness; and let Thy saints shout for joy," which it will be remembered was the text upon which he preached at the dedication of the Metropolitan Church.

On the 17th of June he was permitted to rebuild his home, and was married by his friend, Rev. Gervase Smith, to Miss Mary Foster, "the

CITY ROAD CHAPEL.

friend of many years, and of the dead." He adds, "For this great mercy I desire to render thanks to a merciful God." He could not live without a home, and in his wife he found an affection deep and enduring, and a ready, helpful sympathy, which he sorely needed, and which were an unspeakable comfort to him during the remainder of his life. God comfort the widow; for since her irreparable loss the world can never more be the same to her.

The Conference appointed him to Warwick Gardens, Kensington, a circuit with but one chapel. Whether his health would be equal to the regular round of circuit duties was still an experiment, but he was given an assistant, and he entered upon the work with "an earnest purpose to devote himself fully to Christ, and to labour for the salvation of souls." After a position for five years of such high distinction and commanding influence, his new sphere must have seemed cramped and limited, but he had abundance of work on his hands, as he was also chairman of London Second District.

The following letter, written to me after he had got fairly in harness, tells how his time and thoughts were engaged:

MY DEAR FRIEND,—The day is too short for its work.
10

I feel this continually, and never more so than now. I
have purposed to write to you for a long time past, but
have been "let hitherto." I do not wish you, however, to
consider that my affectionate interest in your welfare is
one whit abated. I was delighted to receive your last,
and to hear of your prosperity and success. May the
Lord make you yet more abundantly useful. My work
here is hard. My chapel gets crowded in fine weather,
but there is a difficulty to upbuild the Church, the living
Church. The place has been built 12 years. It is about
like Elm Street, and it has never been a success. It is
in an aristocratic neighbourhood, where Romanism, and
Ritualism, and High Churchism, and many other "isms"
abound. When I came there were *seven* pews let, and
only about 150 sittings altogether taken, eighty members
in the church—none wealthy. We have already increased somewhat—have let as many more sittings, and
are not without encouraging tokens of the Master's
presence. I hope I shall see you before I leave Kensington. Your education is not complete until you have seen
England. I gave the "Mayflower" in Exeter Hall last
night. The Y. M. C. Association resuscitated their
winter lectures with an experimental course of eight,
which I last night opened. The hall was crammed to its
utmost capacity, and it was like a heated oven. I am,
by consequence, not fit for much to-day. My boys are
doing pretty well. I fear Morley's desires after the
ministry are not strong. He seems to be losing them,

and I fear some declension in spiritual matters also. Annie Panton is with us just now on a visit. She is very thin, and does not look as well as when in Canada. My dear friend Gervase Smith is the object of much solicitude with us just now. He is very unwell. I trust rest and care will restore him. He has sadly overtaxed himself, as we are all in danger of doing. We are in great excitement about the School Board elections. Our Wesleyan friends are not united, and consequently we have been defeated in Manchester, Birmingham, Bradford, and several other places. They wanted me to run for this district, but I declined. Bowman Stephenson is a candidate for Hackney Division. The elections came off on Thursday. Mr. Charlesworth, of Toronto, is here. I see him sometimes. Annie sends her kind love to you and Mrs. Johnston. Pray remember me most kindly to all the Centenary friends—Sanfords, Listers, Bensons, Moores, Roaches, Mrs. Jackson, etc. I am just called off to dinner, and have to go into the city this afternoon to a sub-committee. These committees plague one sadly. Write to me when you have leisure, and give me all news.

Ever yours affectionately,

W. M. PUNSHON.

The year is closed with this record:

"All praise to the goodness that has brought me through many vicissitudes to the last Sabbath of another year.

'The servant is above his Lord.' I have a home, friends, a sphere of usefulness, power of work, and light to work in, some acceptance with the people, glorified friends linking me with the better land, a living Saviour, a Spirit of Holiness and Power which has not left me to myself, and a resolve to be wholly the Lord's, with a good hope, through Christ, of being preserved and presented to the Father." P. 396.

Early in February, 1874, Dr. and Mrs. Punshon, accompanied by Mr. and Mrs. Gervase Smith, visited Italy, going as far south as Naples. The dream of his life was realized in seeing Rome. Through " a struggling moonbeam's misty light" he visited the Colosseum, and " climbed its steep staircases, lost in wonder and awe, and haunted with visions of the ancient world."

The Arch of Titus, the Palace of the Cæsars, the Forum, the temples and columns, the Seven Hills, with their endless associations, the galleries and museums of sculpture, all are visited and minutely described ; and he closes by recording his gladness "at the opportunity to declare in the Eternal City the gospel of the grace of God."

From Rome he journeyed to Naples, with its inexhaustible beauties, its wonderful suburbs—

ancient and modern—its magnificent bay with islands rising like palaces out of the sea, the girdling mountains, with Vesuvius, a " pillar of cloud by day and of fire by night."

On his return home, he continued in unintermitting labour until the Conference in July. His public engagements were many and heavy. During the first seven months of this year he lectured thirty times, and spoke frequently at missionary meetings, but he was limiting himself to not more than a single service on a single day.

On the 7th of June he makes this record :

"Mercifully preserved through exhausting heat and labour in my missionary deputation. Had a season of intense difficulty on Tuesday while preaching at Brunswick. Distressed by the heat almost beyond endurance, and had a strange flushing feeling, as if the blood were being determined towards the head, which I have had once or twice in Montreal, but nowhere else. The meetings were uniformly well attended, financially successful, and conducted in a good spirit. During my absence I completed my fiftieth year."

Of such immense popularity, his administrative powers trained and strengthened by his

THE ARCH OF TITUS.

service in Canada, it was generally considered
certain that he would be elected President of the
Conference.   And when the Conference of 1874

BAS RELIEF IN ARCH OF TITUS.

assembled in Cambourne, on the 29th of July, by an overwhelming majority of votes he was raised to the highest position in English Methodism.

On taking the chair, in the course of his address, among other things, with characteristic modesty, he said :

" I can truly say that this moment of my honour is the lowliest moment of my life. Any feeling of elation is effectually overborne by the consciousness of personal unworthiness, and by a sense of deepening responsibility which awes me while I try to realize it. I should be ungrateful, indeed, if I were not to express my sense of the kindness of those whose votes have placed me here. Although I humble myself before God in the presence of my brethren, I feel that ever since He called me into this ministry I have had one mark of discipleship—I have loved the brethren. My heart has gone out after them with an ardour which many waters could not quench. I have longed for their esteem as I have never longed for worldly treasure, and as a mark of your regard and confidence in me, this election to-day is a tribute more precious than gold. Of my manifold infirmities I feel a great deal more than I shall say ; but I remember a saying of one of my distinguished predecessors in this office, that every office has its perquisites, and that the perquisites of this particular office are the prayers of the brethren." Pp. 402-3.

The year of his Presidency was severe, on account of its great exertions and heavy cares. He had reached the highest point in his public life, but his health suffered from the effects of continuous sessions of committees, and exhausting connexional labours—the Hymn Book was revised and enlarged, Lay Representation was being discussed, and other great questions affecting the future of the Church.

A letter written to me during his Presidential year shows how incessant were his activities:

MY DEAR FRIEND,—All the fulness of the Advent and New Year's blessings to you and yours. May the skies rain down the benediction from the upper and nether springs. I can't make you understand how difficult it is to find a moment this year for the claims of friendly correspondence, but I beg you not to imagine that my memory of Canada and the "elect" Canadians has cooled, because so few letters find their way thither. Every morning brings me some difficult letters to answer —generally a dozen or more, and by the time they are despatched the morning is gone. Then committees come sometimes in battalions, and all the country cries out to see the President now and then, and so my life is busy, and my friends are defrauded of their letters. Lately we have had an anxious house. You would hear that I had been ill. Since my recovery J. W. came home from Cambridge, ill with ulcerated throat and with rheumatic fever. He went back very feeble on Saturday, and to-day the examinations for the Tripos begin. I am not sure that he will be able to go in, and fear he will have to take an "egrotat" degree. Anyhow he cannot do himself justice.

Morley and Percy are well. I had Dr. L. Taylor calling on Saturday, and Mrs. Varley this morning. She said she stayed with the Listers, in Hamilton. Mr. V.'s church here is suffering somewhat in his absence, and she came for a little counsel and help. I am delighted to hear that you contemplate a visit to the Old World next year. If you leave on Saturday, the 5th of June, and land, as you state, at Londonderry, you will just get to Belfast in time for the opening of the Irish Conference, where I expect to preside, and shall hope first to see you. If you will let me know definitely when you have fixed, and that you have fixed for that time, I will try and secure you quarters in Belfast for some days, and you could make that a centre for excursions in the north. Of course, my presidental duties cease at the opening of our Conference on the last Wednesday in July, so if you wish to see me in the chair, you must be there at some of the committees previously, and on the first day to see the new President elected. Don't try to crowd too much into your tour. It is almost too late for Rome, the season will be so hot. Nearer the time I will write (D.V.) again. But stick to the 5th of June.

Love to your wife, Listers, Sanfords, Jacksons, Bensons, Moores, Rices, etc. I wish I could write some more letters. The Lord have you all in His loving ward.

Yours very affectionately,

W. M. PUNSHON.

In February, he was greatly shocked by the unexpected death of Dr. Wiseman, his warm and deep-souled friend, who had visited him in Canada, and stood with him on the platform of the General Conference in New York, in 1872, as the representative of British Methodism.

He was one of the " men of stature " in Methodism, a prince, and a great man in Israel ; and it was a most trying service, which officially devolved on Dr. Punshon, to deliver the address at the funeral. He was not only subdued and solemnized by the sad event, but felt that the bereavement to the Church would probably affect his own future. It was my rare felicity to be with him in his own home during the closing weeks of his office. No words can give any idea of the heartiness of the welcome he gave me. He was more than kindness, even affection itself. I accompanied him to Sheffield, attended the committee meetings, was at the opening of the Conference, and saw the joy that lit up his countenance when his intimate and beloved friend, Rev. Gervase Smith, then Secretary, was chosen to succeed him. His last official duty was to deliver the charge to the newly-ordained ministers. His counsels were founded upon Acts xx. 28: "Take heed therefore unto yourselves, and to all the flock, over the which the Holy Ghost hath made you overseers." I shall never forget the effect of that address upon the immense congregation. His eloquence seemed to rival all his former triumphant energy, and unction, and power, and the address left on the minds of all who heard it the permanent impression of something reaching nearly to the limit of human genius in sacred oratory.

The vacancy in the Missionary Secretaryship, caused by Dr. Wiseman's death, was filled by the appointment of Dr. Punshon. The work

was congenial to him, and for it he was pre-
eminently fitted. He had, from the day he
entered the ministry, given the cause of missions
his eloquent advocacy. His life on both
hemispheres had been identified with all the
missionary movements of his Church. He had,
perhaps, more than any other man in British
Methodism, come into contact with missionary
work and missionary workers of every kind.
The brilliancy of his endowments were not more
distinguished than his ability in administration ;
for he was diligent, systematic, practical, and
his heart and mind were prolific in measures for
the prosperity and enlargement of the Society's
operations. This office he held for the remainder
of his life; and, as Mr. Macdonald justly observes,
was the fitting climax of his life's work. The
duties, the anxieties, the vast responsibilities of
the department, no doubt exhausted him, and
hastened his end ; but it was fitting that he, who
had been for thirty years the foremost among
missionary speakers, firing the heart of the
Church, and awakening its conscience to duty
toward the perishing millions, should have his

imperishable name indissolubly linked with the *Mission House.*

During the year of his ex-Presidency, the minds of the English Wesleyans were greatly agitated on the question of Lay Representation in the Annual Conference. The momentous question was to be decided at the Nottingham Conference.

Dr. Punshon, whose mind had been broadened by being "abroad," saw nothing but good in the association of lay-men and ministers together, in a representative conference, for the transaction of business of administration and finance, which had been committed hitherto to the mixed "Committees of Review." The consensus of feeling and sentiment, in favour of the change, throughout the connexion was wonderful; but a formidable opposition to it was developed, supported "by the learning and rare personal authority" of Dr. Pope, and the unrivalled constitutional knowledge and debating power of Dr. Osborne.

The debate, which was opened by Dr. Punshon, with a resolution in favour of Lay Representa-

tion, lasted four days. Dr. Osborne, the Nestor
of the Conference, rallied all the opposing forces,
and with his old-time power and ingenuity, and
a mastery of assault, well nigh irresistible, made
his memorable speech on the third day, but it
did not carry conviction, and when the debate
was brought to a close on the following day, by
Dr. Punshon, in a masterly speech, cogent and
mighty in argument, pungent and keen-edged
in wit, happy in illustration, sunshiny, and full
of good-temper throughout, he carried everthing
before him, and his resolution, affirming the
principle of Lay Representation, was carried by
369 votes to 49, a majority of over 300. In a
letter written to me shortly after, the full
contents of which I cannot give, because of its
many personal allusions, he says:

"We had a splendid debate on Lay Representation.
I moved the resolution which affirmed the principle. We
had no idea of winning so decisively. We quite expected
a minority of 150 or 200. In the earlier part of the
discussion, the issue, though not doubtful, was critical,
as to the nature of the division. After Dr. Osborne's
speech, we felt that if we only kept our tempers we were
all right. Olver had been kept in waiting for Osborne.

That was the only little bit of arrangement that we had. It was a time of much solicitude and prayer. And wasn't it a grand thing that, when the vote was announced, 369 against 49, it was received by the winners in thankful silence, not a cheer, not a vaunt ; all felt it too solemn for that. Our committee on details meets the first week in February. We still need much wisdom. Pray that it may be given us. I removed from Holland Road in September, having bought Mr. Boyce's house on his retirement. My place of residence is now in Surrey, about the same distance from the Mission House, but across the river. My house is only two stories and a half, and I have got a very comfortable study on the ground floor. The address is " Tranby Brixton Rise." I am four doors only below Mr. Wm. McArthur, and near his brother Alexander. So we have nice friends at hand. The boys have all been home. John William is still teaching. Annie Panton is coming to visit us in January. They are are all pretty well, as are the friends at Kew, and the Smiths. I will order the *Recorder* for you. The *briefs* are commonly mine, *i.e.*, the leaderlets after the large leaders. I edit it, but I have so large a staff that I can scarcely get time or room to write much myself."

Shortly after this he had a severe bronchial attack, and was much depressed in spirit. He had morbid and frequently recurring fears of death, and with his habit of unwise self-dissection, he was trying to settle the question, whether his warm love of life was sinful or not; trying himself continually by the test, "Would you be willing to die now?" Why should a man be willing to die before the appointed hour? Why should he worry about the love of life, which keeps struggling up even in hours of severe pain and weakness? Why should he not enjoy life intensely, and go bravely on unshrinking unto death?

In March, he started for Italy, to recruit his shattered energies, and visit the mission churches on the continent. He preached in Paris and in Rome; saw something of the work in Spezzia, Bologna, and Padua, and was deeply interested with the efforts made to rescue Italy for Christ. In his journal, on his return, he records the fact, "No fewer than seven ministers have been called away since I left home. The day wanes, and there is much work to be done."

It was the tolling of the bell of time, telling him that another and another had gone on

11

THE LOUVRE AND TUILERIES, PARIS.

before, and that while the day lasted for work, his hands must not slack.

The journal references to ill health, exciting services, nervous fears, and distresses increase, and the biographer says:

"During the later years, there was scarcely a day without its bodily discomforts, or mental depression. Not that he was thereby incapacitated for work, or that there was no happiness for him in his home life. This was far from being the case. But the elasticity, and superabounding energy of former days was gone, and nothing could restore them. Physically, he was reaping what he had sown, gathering a harvest of weariness and pain, from the prodigal expenditure of himself in former years. Something of this was apparent to everyone, but neither himself, nor those who watched him most closely, knew how complete was the undermining of his health, or with what steady course his vital powers were deteriorating.

"Meanwhile he laboured strenuously at the duties of his office, and, during the year, preached between seventy and eighty times, lectured eleven times, and addressed upwards of fifty meetings. He also took considerable part in the management of the *Recorder* newspaper, frequently contributing leading articles." P. 436.

Trouble and suffering were plentifully strewn

along his path, pain and distress were knocking loudly at the door. Yet he was still the inde-fatigable worker, and none realized that his brilliant and useful career was approaching so sudden a termination. But the night was draw-ing near. Still he wrought on strenuously and unceasingly. True, he could not make, as of yore, those mighty orations in the pulpit and on the platform. His style was more subdued; yet, whenever he spoke, men felt the spell-like fascination of his eloquence, and sat entranced and charmed by the force and vividness of the truth that flowed from the lips of the mighty enchanter. His missionary speeches were not so laboured and elaborate, they were statements of finance, appeals to the conscience and to personal duty; but now and then he would pour forth his fervid, impassioned appeals, and bursts of elo-quence, that were unsurpassed even in the full blaze of his unrivalled popularity.

His journal of March 17, 1881, contains the following passage:

"Lectured to an immense crowd on Tuesday at the City Temple. Recalled some of my former feelings for the moment, but my time for this kind of usefulness is nearly over. Shattered nerves demand a quieter mode and sphere of work."

The biographer estimates that he lectured no less than 650 times, to audiences ranging from 500 to 5,000 persons, and that in this way he raised $250,000 or $300,000, for various branches of Christian work; besides giving a mental and moral stimulus to tens of thousands of persons brought under the sway of his commanding eloquence.

In May, he set out for Germany, to visit the missions, and transact important business on behalf of the Society.

In June, he accompanied Dr. Pope, the President, to the Irish Conference, which met in Dublin; and at the first Representative Conference, entered heartily into the proposed scheme for the Thanksgiving Fund. The rest of the year was given to the advocacy of this movement, which, under the vigorous and unfaltering leadership of Dr. Rigg, the Conference President, was carried to a triumphant issue. It was proposed to raise a million dollars. The

lessness, prostration, loss of appetite, and nervous fears.

The last Conference he attended, the Conference of 1880, met in old City Road Chapel, London. To Dr. Punshon, the most gratifying incident in connection with the gathering together of the brethren, was the meeting with his boyhood friend, Richard Ridgill, from Africa, after a separation of forty years. Those who know how strong and tender was his affection for his friends, can understand with what warm grasp of hand, and glance of kindling eye, would he welcome, as guest to Tranby, his old and dear friend; and with what tender and unselfish care, with what kindly and graceful ways, he would contribute to his enjoyment during his stay in the home-land.

The year closed in weariness and anxiety over his eldest son, John William, who was daily sinking in consumption. Still, oppressed with anxieties, painful apprehensions, there was no respite from the labours and duties of his administration. He toiled at the desk, sat in committees, travelled, preached and lectured, as

actual amount raised was nearly a million and
a half dollars.

The following summer, accompanied by Mrs.

ITALIAN SWISS VILLAGE.

Punshon and Mr. and Mrs. May, of Clifton, he
renewed his acquaintance with the snow-clad
Alps, drinking in the majesty and beauty of
mountain scenery. But he suffered from sleep-

few men in the most robust health could have
done. " Besides fulfilling his manifold duties at
the Mission House, he preached sixty-five times
during the year, visiting almost every part of
England; lectured thirty-five times, and addressed no less than sixty-one public meetings,
most of them on behalf of the Missionary
Society."

On January 26th, 1881, his journal records:

"Another stroke has fallen. I am again bereft. My
first-born son, the object of so many fond hopes, deep
anxieties, and fervent prayers, died at Bournemouth to-
night, at 6.45. May this sorrow move me to a deeper and
holier consecration. My Lord and Saviour, Thou who
hast redeemed me and mine, four of whom I trust are
now with Thee, hear and accept my vow."

Two days after, he writes of the beautiful
clay : "It was the face of an angel that seemed
to smile upon us from the coffin, so exquisitely
carved were the marble features, and so heavenly
the upward aspect. I am greatly comforted in the
thought of the wonderful change which affliction
wrought in his feelings and sentiments toward religion. He loved his Bible intensely, and scarcely

read anything else. He tired of all trifling conversation, expressed himself, even in moments
of deep personal humiliation, as clinging to
the Rock, and his last articulate word was
'Jesus.' "

The writer reached London in impaired
health, about the time of Dr. Punshon's bereavement, and wrote to him at Bristol, where
he was spending a few days with his chosen
friends, the Mays, intimating his intention of
crossing the Mediterranean to visit Egypt and
the Holy Land. He replied, suggesting a quiet
stay in the South of England for six weeks or
so, and then a journey with him to the Pyrenees
and the South of France. At any rate, he insisted that I should not start for the East until
his return to London. Accordingly I delayed,
spending a few days with our noble friend, Rev.
Dr. T. Bowman Stephenson, of the "Children's
Home," Bonner Road. And when on Saturday,
the 5th of February, I went over to Brixton,
I found Dr. and Mrs. Punshon at home, and
awaiting my coming. He gave me a most
tender and cordial welcome. I noticed his worn

and shattered aspect, and he was saddened by
grief. His physicians had insisted upon his
taking rest, and I began to urge him to accompany me to Jerusalem. His spirit kindled
at the thought, and we began to plan our journey; but, as Senior Secretary, he assumed the
full responsibility of the Mission-house; as
Deputy Treasurer he was harrassed and em-
barrassed with slow returns from the circuits,
and was fretting and fearful lest the income
would fall below the expected amount, and so
he concluded that he could not possibly be
spared until the accounts of the year should be
closed, a month or two later. Accordingly, we
arranged that he should meet me in Rome, on
my return from the Holy Land, and that we
would take Northern Italy and Switzerland
together. Those were rare and delightful days
spent at Tranby, the recollection of them is a
most cherished possession. On Sabbath we
attended morning service in Brixton Hill
Chapel, and heard Spurgeon, in his tabernacle,
in the evening.

On Tuesday, the 8th of February, we dined

with Rev. Dr. Hussey, the genial and learned
Rector of Christ Church, Brixton ; and in the
evening, he was greeted with a whirlwind of
applause, as he delivered in the Rector's spacious
chapel, his " Men of the Mayflower." This was
his last lecture, and with ripened eloquence he
depicted the struggles of the Puritans, and the
fury of their oppressors, as they were tracked
through wood and wold, "the baying of the
fierce sleuth-hound breaking upon their seques-
tered worship." As he traced the character of
these " Pilgrim Fathers," their faith, their stern
integrity, and heroic endurance, and rebuked
in clarion tones the sectarian bitterness, deser-
tion of duty, and failure of faith that belonged
to modern, no less than earlier, days ; he seemed
like a brave prophet of old, speaking his burning words to the people. On the way home
from the lecture, I asked him why he had
selected such a subject for an audience made up
almost entirely of Churchmen, who were not
accustomed to hear much about the virtues of
the Puritans. His characteristic answer was,
that this age needed to be reminded of them,

that the subject should be of interest to all Englishmen, and that he never faltered in the utterance of his convictions before any congregation. The great audience was enthusiastically responsive, and testified its delight in frequent outbursts of cheers. It was the last public engagement he ever fulfilled, the last time he ever addressed an audience. As I think of him now, standing upon that platform, pouring forth a torrent of splendid eloquence, the hearers rapt, spell-bound, electrified, a thousand associations rush upon me, and the tears come into my eyes, as I recall the tones of his voice, the flash of his eye, his burning enthusiasm, and overpowering impressiveness. His last public utterance was given, though only the Master knew it.

That was a memorable week. Some portions of each day were given to sight-seeing, and it was no small thing to see through his eyes such historic places as City Road Chapel, Bunhill's Field, St. Paul's Cathedral, and Westminster Abbey. Sir William McArthur, his intimate friend and neighbour, was at that time Lord Mayor of London, and the hospitalities of the

Mansion House were cordially extended to us, so that on more than one occasion we met in the drawing-room of the lordly house of the city's chief magistrate.

MANSION HOUSE.

The evenings were spent in his study, the bright and cheerful centre of his home-life, where we chatted with his wife and fond niece, Miss Edith Gresham, to whom he was the one object of love and devotion ; examined his rare collection of autographs and treasures of cabinets and albums, and always, before retiring, we had long conversations about the work in Canada and friends and workers there. He had a royal faculty for remembering names and identifying ministers. We would go over the roll of the Conferences, and mark where death had thinned the ranks. He seemed to have a personal acquaintance with each minister of the Conference over which he used to preside, and would enquire after the success, not only of the more prominent, but of the more slenderly gifted and obscure. He was singularly free from unkind or uncharitable speech; and while incapable of detraction, he tried to recognize everything that was good in each. Especially did he inquire after the character and qualifications of the younger ministers, and who were likely to make their mark in the future.

How sincere and unaffected was his love for the brethren. His signal greatness was in his character rather than in his transcendent gifts —his truth, his goodness, his modesty and humility, his deep spiritual sympathies, the living earnestness and sincerity of the man.

" His heart was pure and simple as a child's
Unbreathed on by the world ; in friendship warm,
Confiding, generous, constant."

A week of refined and genial hospitality soon
passed ; and on Saturday, September 12th, I saw
him off to Walsall, where he had an engagement
to preach on the Sabbath, and myself took the
train for Dover. We parted, expecting to meet
in Rome.

And this brings us to the last entry re-
corded in that journal, so faithfully kept for
twenty-five years. Biography is intensely personal, but these journal extracts have certainly
given a gloom and sadness to the story of Dr.
Punshon's life. For while they reveal the intensity of his religious emotions and convictions
and the depth and reality of his inward spiritual
life, they also show a brooding introspection and
self-anatomizing that is unhealthy. Knowing
something of the firmness of his faith, the
strength and beauty of his Christian character,
the genial, helpful, sunshiny influence of his
piety, one can only account for these morbid
elements which mar the records, from the circum-

stance that they were written during intervals of repose after the most exhausting exertions and at times of enforced pauses from sickness and bereavement; and though they are the outpourings of his deepest and most inward experiences, yet they have caught the sombre tinge of his own immediate environments. Bear in mind, also, that the feelings expressed are more for God's eye than for man's, and that this self-scrutiny, to which he subjected himself, was conducted as in the presence of the Searcher of hearts. His piety was virile and cheerful. His popularity never spoiled him in the least, he was genial and gleeful as a child; and the sorrows which eclipsed his life, for the graves of his household were in both hemispheres, never turned the sweetness of life into gall and bitterness. He was not a melancholy man.

Here is the closing entry in his journal, upon which I looked with tearful eyes the day after the funeral, when Mrs. Punshon opened his private drawer.

The entry was made February 20th, a few

days after his return from Walsall, where he had been taken, in the middle of the night, with sudden and alarming illness, and was unable to preach on Sunday :

" My health is suffering much from reaction, after my long suspense and recent sorrow. Went last week to Walsall, to fulfil an engagement, and had so sharp an attack that I was unable to preach, and now am enjoined absolute rest for some time. I feel all the symptoms of declining health—am much thinner ; my digestive apparatus is entirely out of order, and there is a fearful amount of nervous exhaustion. I am in the Lord's hands, and in my best moments, can trust Him with myself for life or death. But I am weak and frail. My languor makes me fretful, and my unquiet imagination often disturbs my faith. I feel that I must go softly. I should like, if it be the Lord's will, to serve the Church of my affection yet for ten or twelve years ; but He knows what is best, and will bring it about. Oh ! for a simpler and more constant trust—a trust which confides my all, present and future, into my Father's care."

He had been prematurely forced into eldership. His work on earth had been to promote the glory and honour of his blessed Saviour. He realized that he was not yet an old man, and

12

though incessant activities in the Master's service " had eaten him up," still so eager was his spirit to complete his earthly work that he would fain have lived longer, yet he was perfectly resigned to the Father's will.   The Lord and Master whom he loved, who " knows what is best," was calling him from the labours of the Church below to the higher service of the Church above.

About the same date he wrote to me a letter, which I received in Jerusalem, saying that he had had at Walsall a sharp attack of the old trouble of difficulty of breathing, accompanied with great disturbance of the heart's action; that he had been obliged to cancel all his public engagements, that his committee had insisted on his taking absolute rest at once; and that he would start with his wife and son, Percy, about the first of March, on his proposed trip to the south of France.   On the 3rd of March the party left London, spent a few days in Paris and journeyed southward, lingering on the way at Lyons, Avignon, and Nîmes.   They reached Cannes on the 16th, where he had an interview with his life-long friend, Rev. Wm. Arthur, and they talked together about the Missions, the Connexion, the coming Œcumenical Conference, and the interests of the work of God throughout the world.   Mrs. Arthur accompanied him on an excursion on the Estérel mountains, and they visited the potteries at *Vallauris*, and watched the process of manufacturing in porcelain.   As they noted the potter evolve out of his lump of clay form after form, Dr. Punshon's eyes were all suffused with tears, and he repeated in tones they could never forget the lines :

" Mould as thou wilt the passive clay.".

He was being moulded the " passive clay," and fashioned a " vessel of honour" to adorn the palace of the King.   On the 22nd they started to drive from Nice over the beautiful road to Mentone, but, owing to blasts of winds and clouds of dust, they had to turn back and take the train.   That night, at Mentone, he had an attack of unusual severity, the heart disturbance and difficulty in breathing being aggravated by

bronchial congestion. He had sent me a message
to Rome, that owing to his health, he could not
journey further south than Florence, and I was
to meet him in the city of Flowers.   From his
attack at Mentone he recovered sufficiently to
proceed as far as Genoa, and there he grew
worse.   At Florence I received a telegram, ask-
ing me to come to him at once.   I found him
alarmingly ill.   His usual medical attendant,
Dr. Hill, of London, was telegraphed for, and on
his arrival, the weary invalid expressed a longing to turn his face homeward.   He had a pre-
sentiment that he should not recover, and he
desired, if it were God's will, that he should not
die in a foreign land.   He bore the five hours'
journey to Turin fairly well, but complained of
pain at the back of his lungs.   His physician
found on examination that there was congestion.   For two days he rested and was quite
cheerful, but as the night of the second day, the
Sabbath, descended, his agony became well-nigh
insupportable.

O, the paroxysms of suffering, through that
long weary night, as the seconds lengthened

into minutes, and the minutes into hours, and
the hours seemed like days. When the morning
dawned, though utterly prostrated, yet he could

MOUNTAIN SCENERY.

not give up the idea of making another stage
of the homeward journey. The passage over
the Alps, amid the magnificent mountain scenery,
which he loved so much, acted as a tonic, and

he was alert to catch the ever-varying aspects of nature, although his sadly tender bearing suggested the most painful forebodings to those whose eyes wistfully followed his every movement. As the evening came on, though weary with the day's ride, he decided to go on to Paris, and oppressed and restless, he yet sat in the railway carriage through the long tiresome hours. In the gray of the morning, chill and damp, the patient sufferer rode through the streets of the French capital to the hotel, to which we had telegraphed for rooms. After a day's rest he came to London, reached his much-loved Tranby, walked straight into his study, and with a smile of happy restful satisfaction, bade me lead in prayer and thanksgiving to God for the long journey safely accomplished. His mind at rest, surrounded by familiar and loved objects, he seemed better; and when Dr. Radcliffe and Dr. Hill made a careful examination of the lungs and heart, they were able to hold out some hope of improvement. All this time his mind was full of activity, he was interested in all that was going on around, and

when free from the sharp attacks of his painful
ailment, was bright and cheerful. He suffered
at night in bed from oppressive breathing, and
loved to linger in his study until a late hour.
What conversations we had together. I cannot
recall all that he said, but the impression is
ineffaceable. What tender interest clings to
those evening hours! How precious the privilege
of communion with the great man of God just
before his translation. There was no foreboding
of immediate danger. No one thought that his
end was so near; yet there were expressions so
solemn as to startle me, and I said, "Doctor, you
have no fear of death?" "Oh, no, but I do not
like to think that my work is ended." Activity
was the normal condition of his happiness. His
unabated zeal, and immense labours, had literally
consumed him at an age when many a public
man is at his best. His thoughts were busy
with the work which the Master had for him
here. He had lived intensely, and loved life.
"It is the rapture of living," he said. As I
think of him now in the shining heavens, and
remember those hours of communion, the deep

undercurrent of spiritual feeling, the indescribable pathos of his words, his beautiful resig-
nation, eager for work, yet willing to depart,
his distrust of self and simple trust in Christ—
I feel that the sanctifying Spirit was indeed
making him meet for the immortal inheritance.
He took special delight in prayer, and the
reading of God's word, and was afraid lest he
should manifest any impatience under suffering.

On Sunday morning, the 10th of April, the
last of his earthly Sabbaths, his wife read to
him the Collect, and Gospel, and Epistle, for the
day. His spirit was gentle and devout, and
much unspoken prayer was in his heart. Prayer
was offered for him at Brixton Chapel, and at
the Tabernacle, by Mr. Spurgeon, who also sent
him a message of love and sympathy, bidding
him be of good cheer, and telling him that his
own seasons of illness were times of deepest
despondency. Monday and Tuesday he did not
rise, and there was a sinking of his strength,
though no one suspected any immediately fatal
result. His niece said to him, "Uncle, perhaps
after this illness your health will be better than

ever." He answered, "Yes, but it may lead to an entrance into the better world—of which I am very unworthy; but I expect through the merits of Jesus Christ to enter in." On Tuesday night he rested quite well, for him, and on Wednesday morning, the 13th, his medical attendant found him so much better that he did not think it necessary to make an afternoon call; but as the evening approached, his restlessness became dreadful. He got out of bed, and walked unaided to the easy chair, in which he died. His sufferings were indescribable. There was failing heart-power, and the sound of the Bridegroom's approach fell on his quick and watchful ear. The scene was impressively solemn and tender, as he summoned us around him for prayer, and as we poured out our hearts in supplicating for him grace and strength, he responded fervently to the petitions. In the midst of the overpowering attacks of agonizing pain, and the feeling of approaching death, I said, "Never fear, dear Doctor, you will have an abundant entrance into the kingdom." His answer was, "I do not ask that. Let me only have peace." And then his mind reverting to death-bed testimonies, he added, "My testimony is my life." His colleague, Rev. Mr. Osborne, of the Mission House, called and spent a few minutes with him in prayer and spiritual communion. After midnight the difficulty of breathing increased, and turning to his devoted wife, who had through all his illness watched over him with unspeakable affection, he said, " My darling, if it were not for you, I should ask God to take me out of this suffering ; but for your sake I should like to live." About one o'clock, as the faithful physician was pouring out some medicine for him, he saw a change come over the patient. " Am I going, Doctor ? " he asked. " Yes," was the answer. Then his heart turned to the human in love, and to the Divine in unfaltering trust. His wife in her anguish sobbed out, " O my darling, what have you to say to me ? " His answer was, " I have loved you fondly ; love Jesus and meet me in heaven." His second, now his eldest son, Morley, was with them, but the youngest was absent, and his wife asked again, " And Percy, what message for him ? " " Tell him to meet me in heaven." Then looking upward with rapt glance, his lips repeated, "Jesus is to me a bright reality ; Jesus, Jesus ! " A heavenly smile, as of kindling rapture, then the head drooped—there was silence, broken only by the sobs of a widow, and William Morley Punshon entered into rest. His death was assuredly his own exceeding great reward. But the gifted orator, one of the foremost standard-bearers of the Church, was gone—gone in the maturity and plentitude of his powers—gone in the full tide of his useful- ness, and there passed upward into light, one of the most royal souls that ever left the track of its brightness on earth.

He expired early in the morning of Thursday, April 14th, 1881, within a few weeks of the completion of his fifty-seventh year.

The news of his death fell like a thunderbolt upon the public mind. It was an unlooked-for calamity ; and as the tidings passed with extra- ordinary speed through Europe and America, it everywhere produced a profound impression.

There was a burst of universal sorrow; throughout the Methodist Church there was a grief as
though "one lay dead in every house," and
throughout Great Britain a feeling of something
like national regret.   His praise was in all the
churches, and by almost every section of the
press and every class in the community, tributes
of esteem were paid to his memory.   Expressions
of sympathy poured in upon the bereaved
household from every side.   The funeral took
place on Tuesday, the 19th of April.   There was
a private service at his own house ; and from
Tranby to the Brixton Hill Chapel, where his
remains were first borne, the streets were lined
with an observant multitude, through which the
great procession of mourning friends passed.
The chapel was crowded to overflowing with
ministers and laymen from all parts of the country—a congregation profoundly touched with
a common grief.   The service was conducted by
the Revs. F. J. Shaw, Dr. Rigg, Hugh Johnston,
and M. C. Osborn.   The President of the Conference, the Rev. E. E. Jenkins, delivered the

address, which was marked by extraordinary tenderness, discrimination and power.

When the solemn services were concluded, the funeral procession passed slowly on to Norwood Cemetery. There, as along the whole route, were vast multitudes, occupying every available position from which a view could be obtained, their saddened aspect showing their heart-felt sorrow; and there, amid the most impressive signs of sorrow, affection and esteem, his body was committed to the ground, in sure and certain hope of the resurrection to eternal life through our Lord Jesus Christ.

Impressive memorial services were held in many places throughout England; in Toronto, Montreal, and other cities in Canada, where his loss was felt as keenly as in his native land.

Palsied is the eloquent tongue, the "polished shaft" is broken, the "bright and shining light" of the Church is quenched; but he "being dead yet speaketh." He has left behind him fragrant, loving and endearing memories, a name resplendent and untarnished as the sun, and enduring as time ; for wherever Methodism is known, will the name of Punshon be embalmed in her traditions, and cherished in her imperishable memorials. May this record of his life inspire others to the same tireless and impassioned devotion to the service of our Lord Jesus Christ, to whom " be glory and majesty, dominion and power, both now and ever. AMEN."